HIGH IN THE ANDES
A Spiritual Adventure
Novel

by

William Michael Kaufman

DORRANCE PUBLISHING CO., INC.
PITTSBURGH, PENNSYLVANIA 15222

ISBN # 0-8059-4543-1
Printed in the United States of America

First Printing

For information or to order additional books, please write:
Dorrance Publishing Co., Inc.
643 Smithfield Street
Pittsburgh, Pennsylvania 15222
U.S.A.
1-800-788-7654

The Serpent-Dragon Completes the Circle

Serpent-Dragon Completes the Circle

Contents

PART I
INTRODUCTION

Prologue

The Fantastic Journey

L ooking back, I'd say it was the rhythm that started it all. And now, as then, I can still hear that train vibrating along what seemed an eternal track, clicking systematically where one rail followed another. As I stared out the window, eventually I forgot my destination and became lost in a place of shifting landscapes and horizons. Soon I found myself on a different journey, one that I felt I had taken before. I couldn't remember when, or any particular details, but I knew it just the same, in a way that didn't have to be questioned. But where was I going? I must have known, because it wasn't my habit to travel without a destination. Yet the more I pondered that question, the more it eluded me. I finally let it go (as though the very effort to remember had the opposite effect) and discovered that the act of letting go allowed me to remember; allowed the memory to come a different way.

The memory was not a thought, but a knowing; just *knowing*. Only know as I look back and analyze, I can say that *knowing* is a pure state in which those building blocks of intellect, like doubt, inquiry, categorization, and assessment, find no interplay. *Knowing*—an ineffable state of being—devoid of those building blocks, yet blissful, peaceful, all encompassing. And yet, I later reflected, where is the journey in just the being? My answer was not a resolution but simply the reflection that one was a state of inquiry, the other of *knowing*....

"May I join you?" he asked. How long it took me to shift realities, I'll never know, because where I had just been, the dimension of time didn't exist. Yet in the glance that brought my gaze directly into his eyes in that single movement came the realization that I had known him in some distant and ancient past. Somehow we were beyond, yet prior to, introductions, and our current names now little mattered.

We focused together for a moment out the window on the clouds, which seemed to enshroud us within anther dimension of *knowing*. The pulsing on the tracks became the beating heart that sustained a body of shared memories; a shared love so deep that our souls vibrated as one. Our gazes came back together, and as they met, our hearts embraced, and held ever more strongly as we wondered how long it had been since we were last together, and realized how much we had missed each other.

What the relationship might now become was a thought that would only manifest in a different time frame. For the moment, we dwelt in a timeless rapture and floated past boundaries into a place of engulfing joy. Our souls were as two clouds becoming one and spreading infinitely in all directions.

As the reverie gave way to our more immediate surroundings, my new friend (old self?) extended his hand.

"Winston's the name," he said, "but don't worry, I'm not a smoker," an assurance he appended knowing the section we were seated in. "I get off at the first stop."

Only later would I fathom the meaning of that cryptic statement. For the moment, my mind was still engaged in pursuing the origins of our relationship. Responding to my silence, Winston followed up his introduction with an intriguing tale of his recent trip; a spellbinding account that inured me to its length.

Chapter One

Return to the Mountaintop

"I was hiking and exploring through various parts of the Peruvian Andes with a small group I had connected with in the States. We would drive to different places indicated on our maps as areas of historical significance then explore on foot. At one point our road was blocked with massive amounts of rubble, as though a storm had come ripping through. I thought this was strange because we hadn't encountered any other such disturbed areas, but I seemed to be the only one bothered by this fact. The others were more concerned with returning to the main road. As we couldn't turn around, however, we started to back up, though not without some trepidation, as the road was precarious enough just going forward. We hadn't backed up very far, however, when we spotted a small road way off to the side. While we were relieved to find an alternative to backing up any further, we were equally surprised we hadn't noticed that path on our way up but figured we had been just too concerned with the sharp drop on the other side.

"A short drive brought us to a small site littered with a few ruins. The others in my group, more concerned with finding the sites already listed on the maps and discussed in the guide books, quickly decided to leave, happy to have at least found a way to turn the jeep around and drive forward. Something about that place, however, hooked my attention more than the official ones. I knew I needed to stay and explore further. This was a golden opportunity, I figured, to part their company. It had already become apparent earlier in our trip that our interests diverged. While theirs centered around the delight of verifying texts with direct observations of ruins, I felt myself being pulled into another time period. While the others perceived ancient foundations upon which they superimposed the walls from composite pictures, I saw—no felt!—the activities and the lives of people interacting in and out of those walls. Yet to use the word 'felt' doesn't adequately describe my experience. It was not the experience of feelings one normally has, nor ones I had ever had. I felt transported, as if I were back in a place where I had lived before.

"After what I was told was fifteen minutes of shouting my name by members of my group eager to move on or they would just leave me behind, I decided now was the time to go my own way. I told them we'd meet the following day at our next destination, and if I didn't show up, they should just move on without me. This would give me the opportunity to explore without interruptions.

"I was now completely alone after my group left, and I began to explore the area. Twilight soon set in, along with fatigue from the day's hike. A boulder I eyed at the edge of the foundations invited me over for a rest, and I heartily complied. An intense stillness filled the void of these toppled monuments. A peace overcame and comforted me, like slipping into a warm whirlpool.

"Perhaps I dozed off; I wasn't sure of anything anymore. Anyway, after a while, something caught my attention. Something moving. I looked up, and in the lingering light, I saw a shadow moving between two pillars. I figured they must have been trees, because all the pillars lay strewn in pieces on the ground. I didn't dwell on that point, however, because I noticed a succession of these shadow-like figures following the first. I looked on spellbound until I had counted almost a dozen of them. Then they stopped. I thought they might be grave robbers or people out on some cult ritual. Yet they made not a single sound. Moreover, there was absolutely no place for them to hide, as the place was wide open; but they mysteriously vanished. By this time, I was paralyzed with fear yet driven by curiosity.

"I got up cautiously, and began a slow ascent up the incline toward the place I had seen the shadows. Despite my deliberate movements, every step crackled the brush under my feet. I couldn't understand how they had avoided making noise, but I knew I was undone, because now my presence must have been obvious to anybody who was there.

"What happened next was so sudden I couldn't protect myself or prepare for the consequences. The rubble under my feet came loose and sent me flying. I was told I hit my head on a boulder as I fell, and the huge bump on my forehead seemed to confirm that."

"Next stop, Portsmith. Portsmith next!" bellowed the conductor, as he swaggered down the mostly empty car past our compartment. Winston and I gave each other an astonished look, as the announcement brought us back to the reality of the train. It had grown dark outside, and now as we looked out, it was our reflection that greeted us back. Winston continued his story. I took up my expectant gaze, having no idea where his account was going, yet I tingled with an inchoate excitement.

"'So, you're finally back among us now. We knew you would come back eventually,' declared the voice, whose body was still a blur as I struggled to focus my eyes. 'It's been a long time, my friend. While we knew where you were all this time, we had to wait until you decided to return,' said another. I still couldn't make out my surroundings, but then I remembered my fall, and realized I must have been knocked unconscious for a time. I surmised that those who surrounded me now were the same ones I was trying to spy on when my mishap occurred. The way they were talking, I guessed I must have been out for some time.

"Finally I closed my eyes and must have fallen asleep, because when I opened them again, I was alone. I was obviously able to focus this time, because I noticed above me a brilliantly lit object of gold. I moved my eyes and noticed two others just like that, all suspended from what appeared to be a vaulted, marble ceiling. I didn't think I was dreaming and quickly sat up to see where I was. The space around me was large, perhaps thirty by forty feet. At the opposite end was a raised platform that resembled an altar. Around the altar were tall objects like vessels, made of gold, and hanging on the wall in back of the altar were large round objects, like shields, also in gold. The long sides of the building were not solid, but composed of columns. I remembered the columns I thought I had seen before my fall where the shadows had passed. I conjectured I must be in a temple, but I knew from my studies of that area that nothing like that existed; at least not anymore.

"This is really insane, I thought, and figured I must be dreaming. But when a throbbing in my head brought my hand up to examine the bump on my forehead, I realized I wasn't dreaming. I thought I must have knocked a screw loose.

"My confused daze was interrupted by two people approaching the table where I sat. They seemed as if they belonged to the temple, because their dress was equally strange and unfamiliar.

They wore robes of a white, silky fabric that came draped over one shoulder, around the front, up the back and over the other shoulder, turning into a gossamer piece woven in golden threads that hung down to the floor, and was held up by a line of seven golden chains around the arm. Their hair was a shiny black woven into thick braids that came around the neck and rested on the chest. Hanging from the end of the braids was a round, golden medallion. I had never seen such a display of gold in all my life and wondered how safe it could all be with everything so open.

"'Welcome back, Narada, just like you to make a dramatic reappearance.' I wanted to believe they had mistaken me for someone else, yet there was something so familiar about them.

"'The others are very anxious to greet you, but we knew this might overwhelm you at first. It's obvious you're not yet clear about your reality. Perhaps you might first like to freshen up and eat something.'

"'Please tell me where I am?' I asked.

"'You're just inside the temple from where you fell. We came back to the temple when we learned you had arrived, to prepare a proper welcome. You were knocked unconscious, and we brought you inside. Come, we'll show you.'

"The two of them led me outside, and the grounds were just as I recalled them before my fall. I walked over to the place I had rested and clearly saw the temple columns where I had seen the passing shadows. I traced my steps to the place of my fall when I suddenly realized the crackling noise of brush under my feet was gone! *This is most strange,* I thought.

"'Come, let us lead you to the bath house. Everything has been prepared for your comfort. Take as much time as you want, and allow the memories to seep in as your confusion seeps out.'

"They led me to another building, similar to the temple in size and structure; but more sumptuous. In it were three pools of various shapes and sizes, surrounded by fountains and gardens. A fragrance unlike anything I had ever sensed filled the air, along with an inviting tranquillity. The layout did not seem random, or purely aesthetic, but rather created in a way to move one through in a pre-determined order.

"The first bath I slipped into was a totally new experience, dissimilar to anything you can imagine. There were no jets in the pool, as in a jacuzzi, yet, as though it were animated, the water began to caress and massage me. Arms of water emerged to

4

massage my scalp and face. Better than a dozen set of hands, the water snuggled all around me; alternately gentle and firm, the rubbing and stroking slowly dissolved all the aches and pains that my hiking had bequeathed me. Then, as if guided by its own intelligence, the water slowly withdrew its massaging action and motioned me out and into the second bath.

"This bath was no less amazing, but very different from the first. The water was much denser than I had ever felt and seemed to pull me in. It had a very soothing quality which seemed to affect my emotions. I began to feel lighter, as though a weight was being lifted off me. Bubbles seemed to form and pop out of the surface, although I couldn't see or feel any place where water or air may have entered. As the bubbles got more numerous, I felt my lightness turning into joy. They seemed to be little bubbles of joy that danced and played all around me, coaxing me to join in their fun. I began to feel almost childlike and felt I could have stayed all day. Soon, however, the action of the bubbles diminished, and, just as in the first pool, the water motioned me on to the third.

"This one truly made the other two feel like child's play. The water had a shimmering effect I had never seen before. It was composed of swirls, the colors of blue and rose, that seemed to radiate from the water, casting a brilliant radiance in all directions. In fact it seemed impossible to determine where the air met the water, as they merged seamlessly together. The most remarkable thing, though, was that it didn't even feel wet. As soon as I entered, I began to feel a tingling sensation. I seemed to enter into a trance-like state, and my whole sense of who I was began to disappear. The joy I was feeling when I entered this pool turned into euphoria. Vibrations started racing up and down my body, and I went into a state of total bliss. The sense of my own body boundaries disappeared, and I felt as if I were expanding infinitely in all directions. I no longer felt that I was an individual entity, separate from all other beings, but in some way connected with everything else that existed. I lost all sense of time and place and floated within an eternal rapture.

"How long I remained in that state was as unfathomable as everything else that was happening. I soon stopped trying to comprehend any of it and allowed the unique pattern of sensation and mystery that was being woven with every new occurrence to envelop me. I was not led out of this pool as in the first two. When my sense of reality returned to my body and surroundings, I found myself lying on a stretch of lawn. As everything else before it, however, the grass was unlike anything you could ever imagine. It reminded me of lying on an air mattress in the way my body was supported, yet the grass had the texture of satin. It emitted a fragrance that seemed both to intoxicate and whet my senses. I no longer questioned why I was there, nor felt they had mistaken my identity. Everything seemed to be perfect, and I began to anticipate with great joy reuniting with these souls with whom I felt the greatest affinity.

"Where I had left my clothes, I found others in their place. I was never aware of anyone approaching to change them, but that is not surprising, considering the states of consciousness I had entered. These clothes appeared similar to those I had earlier seen the two men wearing in the temple. At that time, the thought—though hardly pressing—flashed through my mind that they must be tricky to put on. I picked them up and discovered they were actually all of a single piece! And then, as if an invisible person were there dressing me, the clothes began to wrap themselves around me.

"These were the most exquisite clothes I have ever worn. They were snug, yet light, and caressed my body like a loving embrace. The golden threads gave them a shimmering look and radiance. Like the finest silk, they delicately flowed with my every movement.

"Precisely at the moment I felt ready to proceed, the same two men appeared to guide me back to the temple. There was a twinkle in their eyes, which seemed both to acknowledge what I was feeling and anticipate what awaited me. No one spoke, yet so much was communicated.

"As we approached the temple, a short distance away, a blazing light radiated from it, as though the sun itself had taken residence. There inside five women and three men stood in a semicircle, a foot apart, each glowing within a brilliant cocoon of light. As I walked in, they formed a circle with arms entwined; my two guides behind me closing it up, myself in the middle. The effect was magical. I began to feel a current of energy circulating around me. I heard a low rumbling sound. The energy accelerated. The sound rose in pitch as the energy circulated faster and faster. Everything seemed to be vibrating. Everyone's features turned into a blur, then a dense cloud, and finally a swirling rainbow of colors.

"When all this activity subsided, it was clear that a major transformation had occurred. Now twelve of us, we were no longer in the temple, but outside, on the top of a mountain high in the Andes. We sat in a large circle around a fire, each on hand-made mats with intricate designs woven into them. Additional mats lay at our sides, upon which were placed an assortment of ritual objects and musical instruments. The rest of the mountain top, which spread wide around us, was barren. At the highest peak in that area, we commanded the view of an expansive region. The air was crisp and clear. Against the deep blue of the late afternoon sky, the color that heralds the approaching dusk, a pair of condors soared majestically in a great arc, as if keeping watch—the whole range of mountains their playground.

"At first, we all sat quiet, with lowered heads, as if in meditation. Finally one of the women began to hum in a firm, but low, voice. It had an eerie quality to it, as though it came deep from within the mountain. As though she had tapped into a fountain of energy below her, the intensity of her voice rose until the humming became chanting. Sounds of a strange language emerged. As if on cue, one of the men began to punctuate her chants with a rhythmic beating on the drum. A second drummer joined in. Another man added his pulsing bass voice creating some mystic harmony.

"The chanting and drumming soon diminished in intensity, reverting to the low humming. The woman next to me lightly began strumming a small harp that had lain next to her. I picked up an exquisitely crafted golden flute and started to play it, creating an enchanting harmony with the harp. Throughout the whole time of our ritual, the fire responded to every change in our energy; starting low, building into a huge bonfire, pulsing, dancing, diminishing. Then a curious change occurred in the fire in response to the lyrical playing of her harp and my flute. It began to build again, but this time it took form. Gradually individual wisps of flame came together, manifesting into the figure of a giant goddess. She was awesome to behold, literally a fiery presence. Her whole body undulated with the melody of the music, while her long flaming arms flowed and waved around the circle, touching everyone of us on the head. Amazingly her touch scorched no one, yet created a golden glow around each of our heads.

"Our lead priestess began her chanting again, this time, however, entreating the goddess with prayers for guidance and protection. The event was extraordinary. As our priestess spoke, the goddess assumed huge proportions, extending three times her height, and, as if the sun itself had descended, turned night into day. The very ground beneath us began to tremble. Her massive stature started to pulsate, sending out waves of heat all around her. After a long period of time, all of us silent and expectant, her fiery trembling diminished. In an acquiescent gesture, her fire became the color of radiant rose. As a divine serenity spread over us, she went around the circle, starting with the priest to my left, and one by one, extended her arms and fashioned a cocoon of her pink light around each member.

"The affect of seeing one after another encased within a glowing egg of light was spectacular. Everyone assumed a divine presence and seemed to grow in size. I anticipated that experience with a quiet excitement, especially with the knowledge that I had the honor to complete the circle. However, it was not to be. Right before the goddess approached the harpist next to me, a huge explosion rocked the entire valley below us.

"Then, all of a sudden, a sweeping wind came out of nowhere, whipping around our circle with increasing speed. I felt my body losing weight and density. It seemed as if we entered some kind of vortex, as everything around us began to blur then disappear. It all happened so fast, I fell into a daze. When the air became calm again, I found myself back in the temple, as before, standing in the middle of the circle composed of the same men and women who had greeted me earlier.

"They all had the most beautiful and serene appearance on their faces, and looked at me with the deepest expression of love anyone could imagine. As I gazed into their faces I saw the same people who had just sat with me around the fire. All of a sudden, however, it struck me that these faces had a much younger appearance. Before I could ponder this further I was embraced by each one of them, who came over in the same order we had been sitting, starting with the one on my left. Each hug delivered a bolt of electricity that both shocked and awakened my memories. Each embrace expressed a love that sent every cell of my body into quivers. I was still far from fully understanding any of these events that had happened to me since my arrival, but at least now I knew we were all deeply bonded in some way. I also had no doubt they would clear up the mystery for me. For the moment, however, this would have to wait until our feasting had gotten under way.

"On the table in the temple, where I had first been taken after my fall, now lay dozens of dishes of hot and cold foods. The aromas were intoxicating, and my eyes danced with my nose in a *pas-de-deux* of exquisite delight. I wondered where all this food had come from as I hadn't noticed it before but figured it must have been brought in earlier during our encounter with the goddess. Only now did I realize how hungry I was and wondered how long it had been since I had last eaten. As though he read my mind, my guide echoed that very thought. I glanced over at him, and the look he gave me pierced deep into my soul and told me that much more would be revealed to me.

"I was invited to begin. What had happened earlier with the clothes immediately repeated itself here. As though an invisible servant were on hand, everything was presented to me as I wished it. The twinkle in everyone's eyes expressed their delight in my look of wonder, as though I reminded them of something that, long accustomed to, they no longer marveled at. My nose and eyes proved faithful harbingers: I tasted food unrivaled by the finest chefs anywhere. Each bite invited my taste buds to dance in merriment and sent my salivary glands into ecstasy. Each swallow seemed to send a message of love to my body that every cell would be nourished according to its special needs.

"My musings were interrupted by one of the priestesses, the one, in fact, who had chanted and addressed the goddess. 'Narada, your return has made this a very special day. The scene you witnessed earlier, over 400 years ago, was the last time we were all together. It was, actually, as a result of the magic you forged from your flute music that set the following events in motion. Brother Carana has offered to tell the story of that evening.'

"Brother Carana, it turns out, was the one who had earlier guided and addressed me. He was also the one who had sung in mystic harmony to the priestess' chanting on that last collective night. We looked to him now from our chairs where we were finishing our feast. While we all expressed the eagerness of attentive school children camped outdoors around a fire, I hooked my expectant curiosity on his words as someone seeking salvation. Carana began the following account.

"'As you know from your grade school books, the lives of our people changed dramatically after the Spanish arrived in the sixteenth century. They were a rough lot who came to plunder and conquer us. They spread malcontent throughout the whole of our empire, turned people against each other, spread new diseases against which we had no immunity and decimated millions. Their greed was insatiable and was exceeded only by their desire to destroy. The most vile of an already brutal lot, they satisfied themselves with the torture of the young and innocent and unborn. They competed in the art of cruelty and prided themselves in the subjugation of a civilization whose advancements baffled their comprehension. We gave them extensively from our treasures, but it was never enough. The hidden potential in our gold and silver transcended their awareness, as, indeed, it did most of our own people. The power of riches they saw in these metals excited in them a frenzy of rapaciousness that no one had ever seen. Like some great force of nature that has unleashed its fury, their driving, drunken rage consumed everything in its path and was not to be stopped until it saw its fury spent.

"'The inherent power of our gold and silver was a new knowledge for us. Actually, just some of us. In fact only twelve people had learned their secrets. Historians who later wrote about our social system described our various classes of citizens—farmers, artisans, warriors, government clerics, ministers and rulers, and, finally, our religious leaders. What they never knew, however, and therefore could not write about, was our religious hierarchy, or, rather, dual-function religious order. To them it was all one. In actuality our religious order had two components. The larger one consisted of all the priests who interacted with the people, directing their religious affairs, ceremonies, and rituals. They counseled the people and intervened in local disputes to bring peace and harmony. This component of the religious caste had a rigid hierarchy, with power increasing as one moved up the line. Those at the top wielded a great amount of power. They rarely interacted with the populace, but were more involved in aspects of governance, and, I might add, intrigue.

"'The other, smaller religious component comprised twelve people, six priests and six priestesses. This was a very secret group, known only to the rulers and to a handful of the other top religious leaders. The mission of this smaller *Group of the Esoteric*, as they were called, was to commune with the gods and goddesses, divine their intent and meaning of the natural forces they wielded, and pass on this knowledge to the civic and religious leaders. Some of the intrigue of which I spoke eventually and unfortunately impacted negatively on the *Group of the Esoteric*. A few members of the other religious component, consumed by their envy in the misguided perception of privilege or connection the *Group of the Esoteric* had with the divine powers, betrayed the *Esoteric* to the Spaniards; the consequences of which I'll come to shortly.

"'The direction of destruction of our people by the wrath of the Spaniards had become clear. The *Group of the Esoteric* brought instructions from the gods to the civic rulers regarding a strategy of intervention and attack. The religious leaders, seizing this as an opportunity to enhance their own status and wield greater power, denounced the strategy as ultimately self-destructive to the rulers. It became all too obvious to the *Esoteric* that the chaos the Spaniards brought to our shores had spread like their other diseases to the core of our civic and religious operations.

"'Now motivated by their very survival, the *Group of the Esoteric* gathered on the top of their most sacred mountain to ask their Supreme Goddess for her protection, guidance, and wisdom. Never before had they been so bold in petitioning a divine entity so exalted. Informed beforehand by lesser gods that only through the attainment of a sufficient threshold of energy would they even be able to contact her, the priests and priestesses had never even contemplated approaching her for fear of provoking her fury. Although their only option now, they dreaded the outcome. On the mountain, their meditation and chanting assumed a depth never previously attained. The head priestess began with a petition to the Earth Goddess for strength and direction. Others joined in, with voice and drums. Then...the music magic! First the harp, then the flute: a priestess and priest, a pair of love birds— celebrated among the *Esoteric* for their songcraft—played as if possessed by the gods themselves and filled the air with an enchantment never before heard. A summons so enticing, it brought the Supreme Goddess immediately to the group. She burst forth in a blazing fury and a monstrous size. So enraptured by the song, and enthralled by its players, she saved them for last, intending to bestow a special protection and gift as a reward. However, this was never to be.

"'Just before reaching them, a tremendous explosion rocked the valley below. The force of the blast was terrifying. Instantly the Goddess vanished, her disappearance consuming the very last spark of the fire; even the embers turned cold. Instantly all was plunged into darkness; the ground trembled, and everyone was thrown backward over their heels, cast into a stunned stupor. When they finally collected themselves, they made a horrific discovery.'

"Although Carana narrated the account in the third person, I realized before he finished that the scene they had earlier taken me to witness was the one on the mountain top, that we were the *Group of the Esoteric*, and that I was the flute player. By now they had all cast their expectant gaze on me in anticipation of whatever recollections might play across my face. At that point, if I were still capable of registering anything other than utter amazement toward everything that had happened to me, it was an anxious curiosity concerning their horrific discovery. It was either that look, or the ability he had already demonstrated in reading my thoughts, that prompted Carana to continue his narrative.

"'By now you know how we all come to be together, Brother Narada, although not how you and one other came to be separated. The power of the blast caused a collapse in the mountainside. You, our beloved flute player, and your love mate, plunged to your deaths. It was only because the Goddess had already encased the rest of us in her bubble of light that we were saved. Ironically, what we believed was her intention to favor you two by saving you for last resulted in your demise; a fate, you'll come to learn, that was actually necessary for your own spiritual development. Nevertheless, these were things we only came to learn after some considerable time. For a long period, devastation over your loss dominated our emotions; anger weighed in when we learned how and who caused it.'

"Here, seeing questions dance across my eyes, as well as the desire to voice them, Carana paused, taking the opportunity to freshen his throat with a drink whose origins I couldn't begin to imagine, and whose effect to stimulate and revitalize the mind and body had to be unknown anywhere else.

"'Who was my love mate and harp player?' I asked. 'Where is she now? What caused the explosion? What did you all do afterwards?' Delight twinkled in the others' eyes in response to my curious excitement. Before I could trip over too many questions, Carana responded.

"'Narada, there is much you want to know and much more you need to know. There is a very special bond among all of us, your spiritual family, and a reason why you have now come back. We have waited, as you know, a long time for your return; yet we are still not complete. We have amassed a tremendous amount of knowledge, and have learned to do extraordinary things. Despite all this, for certain reasons, we cannot attain the next level until all twelve of us are together again. On a more personal level, your own progress depends on finding Adonara. We hope that, in the meantime, you will decide to stay with us for a while. Perhaps you will learn what you need in order to find her.'

"This wasn't the response I had expected and, more than anything else that had happened to me since my arrival, threw me into a state of profound confusion and bewilderment. That my questions weren't readily answered was not a thought I immediately entertained. I wondered if this just wasn't my most fantastic dream that I would relish in retelling. Carana only added to my consternation with his next statement.

"'No, Narada, you're not dreaming. But you are overwhelmed. You need to rest and process some of this before moving on. Let us show you to your room, and when you are ready, we will continue where we left off.'

"I was brought to a room, but was too overcome with confusion and fatigue to observe anything about these arrangements. By this point, I just accepted that whatever it was, it was going to be extraordinary and amazing and beyond anything I had ever experienced. Just as I lay down to sleep, however, it occurred to me that Carana had used the name Adonara. I tried hard to think what it was, then remembered he said, 'On a more personal level, your own progress depends on finding Adonara.' Was that the name of the harpist, my former love-mate? And if so, what was my connection to her now, and why did I have to find her?

"It was in the middle of these ruminations that I fell asleep. I have no notion how long I slept. It was way past sunrise when I awoke. Oddly, my watch had stopped functioning, and for some strange reason, the dial kept flashing 12:00, as it does on electrical appliances that haven't been set after a power failure. I felt super-charged, beyond what my deep and sound sleep would normally have given me. Then I recalled the vivid dream from which I had just awakened.

"In my dream, I was on a long journey, going by train. I was by myself, staring out the window, when, all of a sudden, a stranger just appeared across from me. It was a stranger in more ways than one; certainly nothing quite human, and seemingly devoid of any gender identification. The stranger didn't even appear to be fleshy. Rather its surface seemed like transparent plastic, through which pulsing beams of light emanated, casting off a glow that visibly radiated in all directions. It was non-menacing, and, in fact, I felt myself strongly drawn to it, although not in the manner one might normally imagine. Instead its force field, like a powerful magnet, seemed to have the affect of aligning all the particles or elements in my own body. I began to feel a sense of coherence, as though things within me were lining up, enabling energy to move more freely throughout my system. I felt a tingling sensation and a movement of energy from the base of my spine upwards to the top of my head. I began to feel expansive, as though I was larger than my physical body, and my consciousness extending beyond it.

"Soon all the objects within my visual range started to lose their hardness; their edges seemed to disappear, and their surfaces, no longer impenetrable, invited me to go inside. As I did so, I actually felt as if I were going into outer space, into a deep void of distant stars and galaxies. I moved effortlessly through this dark and weightless soup of particles and eventually became aware that the darkness was giving way to light, as though dawn itself was arousing the night out of its slumber.

"As the light brightened, a landscape opened up before me: a desert with the shadows of distant mountains on the outskirts—a broad and empty expanse of lifeless sand, littered only with skeletal remains. Moving over the area, a spot of green I thought was an oasis came into focus. As I approached, much larger than I initially calculated, the oasis appeared to be a tropical paradise, with sprawling gardens, natural water falls, and exotic plants and flowers. I expected to encounter people enjoying these delights, but the place seemed devoid of all human life. I stopped to rest and allow my senses to become intoxicated. I had drifted off, feeling light, when I became aware of sweet, melodious sounds that penetrated the otherwise serene environment. In that period between semi-sleep and waking consciousness, I thought I had dreamt or imagined the sounds when they appeared again. I listened attentively, and distinctly heard the sounds of strings being plucked. I got up, calculated the direction of the notes, and moved toward them.

"As I got closer, the quite audible notes flowed easily together, creating a most beautiful melody. It wasn't joyful, however, but, instead, had a sorrowful quality about it, like a lament. It deeply moved my heart, and I was anxious to see who it was that was so afflicted. My next step brought me in line with a clearing in the leaves, and I saw the most exquisite woman I had ever seen, sitting sedately on the ground against a palm tree and stroking a small harp. Adonara! This had to be Adonara, and I knew it with all certainty. I was mesmerized by her charm and frozen with awe.

"She continued to play, completely unaware of my presence. I wanted to get her attention without frightening her and made noises by breaking some undergrowth with my feet. As this didn't work, I moved to another area so she could detect my approach. I moved closer and softly called out her name, but she still didn't look up. I felt an extreme emotional agitation; a tightness in my chest so intense I feared my heart would snap. I inched closer and closer, until finally I was right next to her. I extended my hand and laid it on her head. Instead of coming to a stop and resting on her hair, however, my hand continued to move through her head, as though it were a mere shadow. I became agitated with terror and dread and began moving my arms wildly through her whole body. But she continued as before playing the same mournful melody.

"That's when I woke up. I was anxious to find Carana or one of the others to relate my dream and find some meaning. I left my room and went to the temple, expecting someone to come up to me on the way. As that didn't happen, I figured they were all inside, awaiting my appearance as before. Yet I found the temple deserted. I explored the grounds but found no sign of anyone anywhere. I started to return to the temple when I became aware of a raging hunger. When I got back to the temple, an enticing spread of food was laid out on a side table. I was somewhat mystified, because I didn't recall seeing it previously. Nevertheless, everything about the situation invited me to stay and eat, and I did so joyfully.

"I figured the time and space were given me to sort things out, digest everything that had recently happened, and wonder what I might do next. The baths I had enjoyed earlier seemed like a natural place to start this process. While their amazing properties were not new to me now, they were, however, no less extraordinary. They seemed to clean more than just the surface of my physical body. Somehow I felt every aspect of my being becoming clean, light, and refreshed. I became more clear about my life and the direction it was taking. I began to recall recent events in my life and observed how they organized themselves into a definite pattern.

"Obviously there was no coincidence about my having come to this place. I had arrived at a crossroads in my life. Not that things weren't working out for me. On the contrary, I had a job that was good and indicative of a promising career. I had a nice place to live, wonderful friends, and a supportive family. Moreover I had the implicit support of basic social values. In other words, everyone encouraged me in the life I was living. They had my whole future planned out for me, including how I should design my career path, my social direction, my living situation, the organizations I should join, and the networks I should develop. I saw my life advertised on the radio, the television, in magazines, and on billboards.

"Yet something in me was deeply disturbed by all this. Something felt missing, and none of the support or signs that I was on the right road to success were able to compensate for the inner hole; a missing piece so large that the greatest success, as imagined by anyone throughout my support network, could fall into one tiny corner and disappear. A voice long forgotten would cry out in those moments when I let go of pursuing other people's dreams, or, at least, that's when I heard the voice. It echoed loudly throughout that inner hole, creating a reverberation that rocked me to the very core of my being. Whose voice it was I never quite knew. I did come to realize, however, that if I didn't listen, the inner hole would only grow, eventually consuming all of myself, until I became just a hollowed-out shell.

"About this time, a curious event, or, rather, series of events, occurred in my life. One Saturday, like any other, I began my routine with my morning meditation. I generally followed this with a light breakfast, a look at any bills needing attention, then an attack on my typical weekly tasks, such as cleaning and shopping. My intention was to get all of this out of the way so I could start my weekend of unencumbered fun. This particular Saturday would be different, however, and nothing of the normal would follow my meditation.

"At the end of the meditation, a strange thing happened. I felt what I could only describe as the core of my being begin to open. I started to have an overwhelming feeling of joy, as I had never experienced before in all my life. I realized that until that moment, the best I had ever felt was something akin to happiness. Now, however, this joy spread throughout my entire body, and I felt electrified by it. Revelations about the nature of the universe popped into my mind. I felt an expansiveness in my being, as though my body couldn't contain my awareness, which now extended outward beyond my physical confines in all directions.

"I decided to leave my apartment and go for a walk, feeling that my rooms had become too small to contain my energy. I headed for the local park to escape the traffic noise and find some serenity in a more natural environment. I walked with a power totally foreign to me, radiating the joy I felt, and making deep connections with everyone I passed. In my meandering, I passed directions for a historic marker that I had never noticed before but decided to ignore it after seeing it had religious associations. I had not gone ten feet beyond the sign, however, when some inexplicable force pulled me back and compelled me toward the marker. Winding around a steep curve in an obscure corner of the park I abruptly confronted a huge monument. Prominently displayed among its inscriptions was a date whose month and day corresponded exactly with my birth date. The voice of my revelations told me to keep this in mind, for its significance would be revealed to me at another time.

"The following week I picked up a local newspaper at a neighborhood store. I had seen this paper dozens of times in the past but never before felt inclined to examine it. This time, as though guided by an invisible hand, I automatically reached over and took a copy. Leafing through it, I came across an ad from some people inviting others to join them on a hiking tour in South America and also inviting their suggestions on particular places to go. As this sparked some personal interest, I went to the library looking for information. Choosing randomly one of three guide books that were on the shelves, I scrutinized the pages in search of pertinent information. Nothing extraneous had been written on the pages until I got to the section on holidays. On that page someone had encircled the date of a Peruvian national holiday and drawn a vertical line on the margin for emphasis. Once again the date coincided with my birthday. Recalling the voice I had heard in the park, I combined all the recent and strange incidents in my life with my need to address an inner calling and decided to get in touch with those people from the ad.

"Delighted with my response to their ad, these people wholeheartedly invited me to join them and welcomed my suggestion that we go to Peru. As it turned out, they were only looking for one additional person, and they hoped it would be someone interested in that country. The match seemed perfect, and we made the plans that, as I narrated earlier, brought me to our eventual separation, and to my encountering the temple and its inhabitants.

"Recalling all these events while enjoying myself in the baths, I decided I was only at the beginning of my journey, and that too much had happened for me just to pick up and leave. I realized that I had begun to tap into that place of emptiness in my life, and that if ever there was the occasion and possibility to fill it, it was now. I left the baths and headed back toward the temple, figuring I would just wait for them there, knowing they, or at least one of them, had to come back eventually. I also thought it's a good place to find some food when my hunger strikes again. I was surprised, therefore, when I arrived at the temple to find all of them sitting around as before, as though they were waiting for me.

"'Hello, Narada, we are delighted you have decided to remain with us for a while. As soon as we were informed, we all rushed back to celebrate the good news. Although we facilitated your arrival here in the most minimal way, it really had to be your decision both to return and to stay.' In this way I was greeted by the same woman who had addressed me earlier. While I also recognized her from our earlier flashback scene as the head priestess who summoned the goddess, I still didn't know her name. 'What do you mean you facilitated my arrival?' I asked.

She responded first to my thought, then to my question. 'My name is Ardana. Do you remember right before your arrival when you were driving around with your companions? At one point you came to an impasse and had to turn back. You were astute enough to observe the anomaly of those conditions. That's when you noticed the side road that brought you here. We created those conditions. That is we blocked the road so you'd have to come back, then opened up the side one.'

"'Why,' I asked, 'didn't you just open up the side one, so we wouldn't have to negotiate that treacherous backward drive half hanging over the cliff?'

'Your companions,' she responded, 'had become so glued to their maps that they just couldn't contemplate any alternatives. This was the only way they would have considered taking anything off the beaten path. The gulf between your apparent adventurousness and their crippling fear had widened to the point that your separation from them was inevitable. They outnumbered you and reinforced each other's fear. They weren't ready, in terms of their spiritual awareness and attainment, to accompany you, and, in fact, your very energy had already stretched them further than they were prepared to go. That treacherous drive, as you so described it, sufficiently unnerved them that they wanted to get back to the mapped roads as quickly as possible.' At this point, Carana interjected a more general statement.

"'Since you will have significant time with us, Narada, we will come back to this incident in the course of our teachings. Doubtless, there are many more things you want to know about, like your dream last night. There are numerous teachings you are ready for, and we are very desirous to impart what we have learned in the last four hundred-plus years. For now let us spend the rest of this day in celebration and in helping you make the proper arrangements that will permit your staying without alarming those you left back home.'

"The rest of that day was very jubilant. I was the center of attention and was held in great esteem. I found this baffling, but, as with so many other things I wondered about, I had to learn that certain explanations come only at their appointed time. I learned the names of the others in our group, and talked with them all. In addition to Carana and Ardana, who had already addressed me, the others were Andora, Arzano, Zarmano, Manora, Balcano, Rolana, Belanin, and Jandara. More than just the intense love they showed me, there was a strong sense of familiarity in being together. The separation in time of nearly half a millennium for them and other reincarnations for me now hardly mattered. It was a homecoming in the deepest meaning of the word: a predominant feeling of pure, unconditional, and nonjudgmental love; a complete and unquestioned acceptance of who I was, all I've done, and everything I've decided.

"I was assisted in making the preparations to extend my time away by Arzano. He procured a phone for me, knowing I still needed one for communication. The arrangements I needed to make went surprisingly easy. For my job, I had already accumulated vacation time, and I was allowed to take it now. Regarding my home, a fortuitous event occurred shortly before I left on my trip. A friend of mine had lost his apartment as a result of a condominium conversion. I let him stay with me, thinking he could remain and take care of it during my absence. He was now delighted he could stay longer. Other friends and family just shook their heads and sighed. It was their belief that I just needed some time to work through my 'emotional' crisis, and they hoped I wouldn't get involved with any political or religious cult. I assured them I was too aware and level-headed for anything like that to happen. I now felt completely free and eager to see how the extraordinary events that had recently so transformed my life would now unfold. It seemed that I had already begun to fill in that gaping hole in my inner life, and, where I had once felt a hollow echo, a joyful excitement now vibrated.

"It was late in the evening when I showed signs of fatigue, and my friends suggested I rest. I might tire easily in the beginning, they noted, as my body was not yet accustomed to the higher frequencies in which they all functioned. Moreover a much higher frequency operated throughout their grounds and buildings, thus permitting the phenomena I had observed. I went to my room, and while weary, the exhilaration I felt did not invite sleep. I took the occasion to examine my room and other buildings.

"My room, like the other eleven, was a separate building. It was oval in shape, with wooden columns on each of the long sides, and solid wooden walls at both circular ends. Golden silk material draped between the columns. There was no visible ceiling, so the whole room was open to the sky. I later learned that an energy force-field covered it instead. All the rooms spread like fingers around three sides of the temple bath; further away, on the fourth side, stood the main temple. Inside the room, there was a round bed at one end and a meditation area at the other. The floor was also made of wood, with inlaid strips of gold forming particular patterns. A strip of silver, about the width of a hand, ran all around the room at the top.

"The feeling inside the room was warm, cozy, private, and intimate, yet also somehow expansive, probably due to the open ceiling. It was the bed, however, that I found most intriguing. It didn't rest on the floor, but, instead, hovered above it! It far exceeded anything I had ever slept in, for, besides being remarkably comfortable, it always let me fall immediately into a deep and restful sleep. Thus did I end my second day with the most extraordinary and loving people I had ever met. My amazement by their accomplishments grew enormously as I stayed with them, and only diminished as I, too, learned their ways."

PART II
TEACHINGS OF THE ESOTERIC

Chapter Two

Bonds

"The next morning when I awakened I realized the sun must have already beaten me by several hours. Just as the day before, the place was deserted. It was rather mysterious the way everyone just popped in and out around there, especially since I never heard or saw any vehicles. I figured I'd avail myself of the accommodations, knowing that eventually someone would arrive. I had my baths then decided to use the end of my room opposite from the bed to meditate.

"I was not new to this, having done mantra meditation for several years. Repetition of a mantra is a way to facilitate anchoring or focusing the mind. Normally our minds are crowded with so many thoughts of all kinds that we're not able to attain any real peace or stillness. By reminding ourselves to come back to the mantra each time the mind wanders, eventually it becomes more focused. After a time, the reminders become less, as does the random firing of thoughts and impressions. One goes into a state of deep calm, expansive awareness, and restful alertness. My experiences meditating were never uniform. It often seemed a struggle just to come back to the mantra or not doze off. Other times if I diminished the random impressions, I would become focused only to invite thoughts of things I was working on. While this proved a great tool to recover things I had forgotten, or get great ideas for some current project, it nevertheless fell short of attaining those higher states of alert consciousness I had heard and read about. I knew this was a question of more practice, so I maintained the exercise knowing about the great benefits to be derived from it.

"I shouldn't have been surprised that the area of the room laid out for meditation was unusual, as everything I had so far encountered was unconventional. The space comprised a scooped out area of the floor like a round inlaid spoon. Several pillows lay in the scoop, but these were not ordinary. You could see right through them. The coverings were transparent, like plastic, but with the feel of satin. Yet it wasn't air inside, because the pillows provided support like foam rubber. In addition—as I learned later, because at the time I didn't have sufficient sensitivity to feel such subtle energy differences—a vertical column of energy rose from the earth, through the scooped-out area, and upward to the sky. Moreover the scoop was designed in such a way that focused the energy from the earth with different intensities on the various chakras, not unlike the way a prism breaks down white light into different colors so they appear one on top of the other.

"While I wasn't at first able to detect this column, I sure could experience its effect. As soon as I sat and adjusted the pillows, I sank into a deep meditation. The problem of calming the mind of random thoughts and impressions never arose, nor did even the need to repeat my mantra. I immediately began to feel a tingling in the area at the base of my spine, then a build-up of warmth. The sensation traveled up my spine, and as it did so, I felt in various places a pulsing of the energy outward. I also felt myself becoming more expansive, as though I encompassed a space around my body. As the energy reached the top of my head, I experienced an incredible joy and felt a deep connection with everyone else in the universe.

"After some period of time, sensations in my stomach of a different sort made themselves obvious and brought me back to body awareness. I decided to head for the temple, assuming I'd find food. Both this and my earlier assumption proved correct, as I saw, standing next to a table of food as though waiting for me, my mentor Carana.

"'Good morning, my dear brother Narada. I hope you had a good night and are looking forward to resuming your spiritual studies. I'm glad you availed yourself of the meditation zone; great way to start the day! I thought I'd join you for a bite as we pick up where we left off yesterday; actually as we left off 450 years ago!'

"After we got some food, Carana continued his account of that terrifying blast on the mountain that separated me from the others. 'As I told you earlier, we were initially baffled that the great goddess we summoned that day on the mountain could not have been aware of the imminent danger we were in, and would have allowed a situation to develop leading to Adonara's and your demise. As it turns out, it was the rest of us who lacked awareness.

"'While it's true that the exquisitely enchanting melodies you and Adonara spun out on your respective instruments enticed the goddess' appearance and secured her favor, she knew something that we didn't want to accept, and she, in her much greater wisdom, was able to execute. When you and Adonara came into our group, you were younger than the rest of us. And when I say younger, I do not mean present life age, although even in that respect, you were both younger. I'm referring more specifically to the soul's age, if you will.

"'The age of the soul pertains to the multitude of human life forms, or reincarnations, a person has had. You see, Narada, each one of us has a soul that's invested with the consciousness, memories, impressions, and thoughts of all its physical existences. Each time you die, you merely give up the physical aspect of the soul, its shell. But since the soul contains all the consciousness from all its life forms, nothing is lost when it gives up the physical body. On the contrary, it gains additional understanding by going through that process. The dying process is the final chapter of the book with your name on it, and every chapter, every page, indeed every letter of every word, increases the soul's level of awareness. Therefore, when the physical body loses the vital life force to sustain it any longer, nothing is really lost, because the greater part of ourselves—the soul's consciousness—remains. Consequently the act of suicide does not necessarily provide a viable solution, or way out, to one's problem or suffering. That's because the consciousness of the problem or suffering, which was experienced on the emotional and psychic levels, still exists, independent of the physical body. There are reasons for our problems and suffering—which we'll explore at a later time—and working through them on the physical plane, including the processes of dying and being born, and the unincarnated states between both of them, is essential.

"'Every soul is a volume of books, a collection of lifetimes full of experiences and interactions with others, from the most significant to the most superficial. With each life we build on the understanding acquired from the lifetimes before, constantly adding to the soul's total comprehension of life. Although the soul contains all this knowledge, much of it is inaccessible to the individual. This is largely because each time the soul incarnates, along with its new body comes a new brain. This organ develops integrally with the development of the body and all its experiences of that particular lifetime. The memory is forged and strengthened with repetition of the numerous events and impressions that engage the body, but doesn't have access to information stored in the brains of previous lives.

"'Nevertheless, while the brain starts each time as a clean slate, as it were, material from previous lives stored in soul consciousness may filter through, especially if the memory comes from an event that made a particularly strong impact on the individual, such as from a severe trauma, or a relationship characterized by extreme hatred or extreme love. This is why it is not uncommon for people to have the kinds of experiences in which they meet someone for the first time and feel they have already met that person, or visit a place for the first time and feel they've already been there.

"'That spark of past life remembering is quite different from normal memory function, and people with higher levels of sensitivity sense that. They notice that a different area of their body has been touched. It can be very subtle, and those with no experience of it might totally ignore it, or translate it into an experience or recognition they're more familiar with. We manage our memory like office files or computer files, creating diverse categories of memory, then sorting the various events and impressions into them, often establishing numerous and complex links or associations among them. Therefore, when an individual experiences something new for which no file or category previously exists, the new impression may just be dumped into a pre-existing file with associations totally inappropriate to it. If, for example, some man has an experience that taps into an impression from a former lifetime, he may either completely miss it, ignore it, or just file it under the *odd, strange or misplaced* files.

"'As I just mentioned, each lifetime adds to our total comprehension of life. There's no real shortcut to this process, except through consciously engaging in spiritual exercises. Because you and Adonara were younger in soul than the rest of us, you still needed a few more physical incarnations until you were ready to advance to higher levels of spiritual attainment. With the much greater wisdom she possessed, the Supreme Goddess did not interfere with your souls' progression and allowed the mountain blast to move you along the process. With greater spiritual awareness, we become less tied to our physical bodies. The human force of physical and ego love can be so powerful people can find it very difficult, if not extremely painful, to be away from their loved ones. This pain comes from the attachment they develop to the physical form, or forms of others. And this is because, as they have little or no understanding or recognition of their own souls, their identity to their own physical bodies and physical existence is dominant. The goddess saw your complete life-stream and each lifetime as just another book in the volume of your soul's library.

"'We eventually came to this realization as well, although we were initially very upset not to have you with us. Or, more accurately, not to have the books titled *Narada* and *Adonara*. As the existence of your souls just continued, we have been in constant contact with you throughout all this time. We have been expecting you because we knew you were ready by having attained the spiritual knowledge necessary to move on with us.'

"'Why is it then,' I asked, 'that you still refer to us by the names we used in those earlier lifetimes? The other thing I am curious about was something you said yesterday about not being able to move on without us. What exactly did you mean by move on, and why do you need us? It seems as if you can do just about anything on your own!'

"'Good questions, Narada, and proof of why you are here. There is a very strong bond among the twelve of us, and it is no accident we are all together. The details belong to a story to be told by someone else at a later time. For now, however, I can tell you that all of us have been together before, and I mean before we were Inca priests and priestesses. Since the rest of us haven't re-incarnated since then, we have kept our names out of a sense of poetry and energy. You will learn much more about energy and its relationship to words and names and all other phenomena. For now, however, since I perceive you are a bit fatigued, let me answer your other question, or at least part of it, before we break.

"'The reason we have remained together for so long is the result of an oath or pact all of us made in the beginning of our association. We vowed to remain together in order to further our growth through mutual support and guidance. We realized early on how our collective energies, when harmonized and focused, had a great deal of power, and how remaining together would enable us to accelerate our spiritual growth, attain great wisdom, and develop our facility with energy. Of course not all twelve of us have always remained together throughout our reincarnations. There have been times other than this current one in which two of us— meaning you and Adonara—have had to take individual paths. Nevertheless, as a result of our pact which was powerfully constituted and blessed by higher entities, we have always come back together. Indeed although the great goddess did honor the dignity of your destiny to close one book and open the next, she also, if you remember, blessed each one of us that night on the mountaintop. And that blessing bonded us ever more tightly together, guaranteeing the integrity of our initial pact. Now we are aware that the time has come again to have our conscious and collective energies focused as one.

"'Let us stop for the meantime, Narada, and continue later this afternoon. It is not good to proceed too quickly in these matters. With every advance in understanding there is a shift in the basic energetic structure of your body. These changes must occur by degrees, or your body would literally be ripped apart. Perhaps an appropriate analogy would be like stretching your muscles, in which the tissues need to adjust and grow gradually into their new position. Take this time to rest, and sit with the teaching. I have to go on an errand, and when I return we can resume.'

"Carana then walked away. After a few seconds I needed to ask him something and started off after him. He was not more than fifteen feet ahead of me but had just turned out of sight as he descended over a hill. When I reached the top, however, in plain view of the slope directly below me, there was not a trace of him anywhere. As there were no buildings or wooded areas where he might have disappeared into, I examined the ground in case there were something like a deep recess, or even a hidden cave, not noticeable from above. Nothing I could find, however, could eliminate my imagining he had just dematerialized himself.

"The sun was already high in the sky, and its caressing rays invited me to lie down on the sloping ground and submit to its warmth. The whole place was so serene, I gladly surrendered to its embrace and succumbed to slumber. I had what I thought at the time was a dream. In the dream, I was walking down a street in an unfamiliar town. It was obviously not a large place, and not very prosperous either. I passed several women walking and chatting together. They were wearing felt hats and brightly colored shawls, and, I gathered, belonged to the local native Indian population. Their faces had the deep creases of an older person, but they walked with the determination and vigor of someone younger. Traces of their Spanish that caught my ear made me think I was in another country in South America. I decided to be bold and ask them where they were headed, but they acted as if I were invisible. I thought I would test that by following them to determine at what point they would respond. We turned off the main road into a smaller one, which at the end curved around and turned into an alley. About fifty yards further was a small wooden house. When we arrived, someone opened the door, as though expecting them, and we walked in. The woman who let us in was clearly young, and as she, too, looked right past me, I concluded I must indeed be invisible to them. I just accepted that as natural and didn't wonder about it.

"'Don Miguel will see you ladies shortly,' said the host. I gathered this was some sort of clinic. We hadn't waited very long when an inner door was opened and a middle-aged man came through the room and out the door we entered. He walked with a slight limp but otherwise had a cheerful countenance and a touch of confident hopefulness. Then Don Miguel himself came to the door to invite the women inside. I looked up and saw that Don Miguel was none other than Brother Carana! He looked right into my eyes, and although he didn't say anything, his eyes flashed a spark of light and his expression communicated that he was delighted to see me. Clearly I was visible to him!

"'Carana, wait, I want to ask you something,' I cried out just as he closed the door behind him. I called out his name again and again, and finally, as though he were at my side, he said, 'Did you have a question for me, my dear Narada?' I opened my eyes and realized that he was standing directly over me, blocking with his body the sun that was now shining on the other side of my face from when I first lay down. I was totally flustered at that moment and wondered if I was still dreaming. I stammered an incoherent reply, but Carana cut right through it in his avuncular manner: 'You're learning faster than I expected, old boy!' he said as he extended his hand to help me up. 'Let's resume our discussion for a little while before we call it a day.'

"Carana continued his explanations as we strolled through the grassy slopes. 'You may have wondered, Narada, why I have initially been more interactive with you than our other brothers and sisters. I'll tell you why. A very long time ago, in an ancient time even before the twelve of us bonded, you and I became deeply connected as soldiers and comrades in battle. We had long philosophical discussions about life and the nature of being when we weren't actively engaged on the field protecting the king's domain. During a particularly fierce battle, you gave up your life in order to save mine. My whole life changed at that moment. All the things we talked about had never seemed quite real, but were, instead, fun, intellectual musings. At that moment, because of your heroic and selfless deed, a poignancy was injected into those discussions that gave them a new depth. With the king's permission I left his service and joined the religious order. I learned a great deal yet always felt something lacking in not being able to share with you and build upon what we had begun. When we met again in a subsequent lifetime I was powerfully drawn to you, without initially knowing why. Then one day, during a particularly deep meditation, a very clear vision came to me. The floodgates of my memory opened up, and I knew with the greatest confidence of our previous connection. You weren't ready then to accept any of this, but knowing how noble your soul was, I vowed always to serve you as guide and mentor.'

"I remained silent for a long time. As Carana spoke, strange sensations vibrated deep within my soul, as though strings from an instrument that had long lain idle were finally being plucked again. Each vibration sent waves rippling through the core of my being. Each vibration sounded a note that tried in vain to form a complete melody. The instrument was rusty and out of tune for lack of use, and I realized it wasn't through struggling I would sound out the tune. Instead the metaphor I formulated suggested the direction I should take.

"'The sun is on the wane, Narada. Let us stop here and watch nature spread her glorious color palette across the sky.'

"We sat down where we were and settled into a relaxed and silent contemplation of the sunset. The colors were indeed splendid and almost mesmerizing as they created within the clouds a dynamic dance of shifting shapes and brilliant hues. As I continued to watch, I felt drawn into that rich tapestry, and, like a painting one has been scrutinizing that seems to come alive, the clouds began to crystallize into recognizable forms and patterns. I didn't recognize it at first, but then the scene of a battle became all too clear. It took on the depth of reality one normally finds in a dream; especially when one finds oneself as both observer and participant. I saw someone on the battle field in a heightened state of excitement, even though the present level of combat had subsided. Although he had absolutely no resemblance to me at all, I knew I was he.

"This 'pre-Narada' came running across the field in that agitated state until he met up with someone who was obviously his comrade. They hugged, and he told his friend that the enemy had retreated and victory was theirs. They fell back separately on the ground in exhaustion, though remained embracing each other's hearts. All of a sudden, hidden amongst the uncut growth at their side, an enemy soldier lunged at his friend with a club. 'Pre-Narada' sprang up with an energy he thought already consumed and caught the force of the club with his head. His friend quickly grabbed the club and made that attack the enemy's last living act. When he turned his attention to his protector he realized it had also been his last act and fell on him with a degree of despair that would make the angels lament. Stepping out of his lifeless corpse a shadow of himself extended a hand on his friend's back and said, 'Zani, don't grieve so. It's really all right. We'll meet again, I promise.'

"The shadow then disintegrated, and I realized that all the colors in the sky disappeared with it. The clouds settled into wisps of gray enshrouded by the deep blue of a retiring day. I looked to Carana for his reaction but he was nowhere around. I began to wonder when he might have left me when I heard the sound of chimes coming from the direction of the temple. I realized I was hungry and he must have quietly slipped off earlier and was now calling me for dinner.

"When I arrived I saw not only Carana, but the others as well, all standing around a very enticing spread of food and eagerly waiting my arrival. Their display of affection toward me remained undiminished, and we spent the rest of the evening in merriment and fun. I hoped to find a receptive opening for a number of questions I had but eventually let go of my need to get answers then, trusting again that I would learn what I needed to know at the appropriate time. Later that evening, just as the night before, I was the first to express fatigue and left the group for my room, anxious for the retreat I knew sleep could provide."

Chapter Three

The Double Incubus

"The next morning was not unlike the day before, except that when I arrived at the temple, expecting to find Carana, I found Ardana instead.

"'Good morning, Narada. I hope your surprise at finding me here is greater than your disappointment!' I protested, but it was obvious she spoke in jest. 'Carana has been monopolizing all your time, so we sent him on his way for the rest of us to have some time with you. Seriously though, you know that he had been your guide and mentor before, and it was essential that he be the first to facilitate your re-affiliation with us. We all have very significant histories and connections with each other and have learned much from the group collectively and individually. We will each spend significant time with you over the course of your stay with us, bringing new teachings and reinforcing old ones. In addition not all of these teachings will take place here at home, but at other locations as well.' After a pause she added, with a gleam in her eye, 'Perhaps you had a glimpse of that yesterday when you visited Carana at a healing clinic in southern Bolivia.'

"Ardana stopped talking for a moment as she saw how this last statement of hers thrust me into a mental struggle. The effort I was making trying to recall my dream yesterday was complicated by a flood of related thoughts: What was the reality of what I saw, how did I manage to see it, what had Carana seen, how did Ardana know about it? Ardana stopped my mental struggle before it became mental torture. 'Don't be alarmed with your experiences up till now, Narada, nor with your inability to understand everything immediately. The progression we make as we move through life and on the road of spiritual attainment never seems straightforward. We would like everything that happens to build upon past experiences in a neat and orderly fashion. While to some extent this happens, it never quite seems so. The pattern that generally seems more obvious is one of slipping back, things not working out as we had intended, realizing we're not where we had hoped to be, wondering why we're back to working on some issue we thought already resolved, and just not making the progress we want or believe we deserve.

"'The reason this seemingly zigzag pattern happens is because we are so multi-layered, and each layer has its unique learning dynamic and manner of processing new knowledge before it truly becomes learned. There is an energy shift that occurs in a particular layer with the attainment of new awareness, which results in a new energetic configuration of that layer. This new configuration causes a disharmony among the other layers. Depending on how strongly the new awareness impacts the layer, and which layer it is, the disharmony is resolved either by moving the other layers toward a new energetic configuration or shifting the one initially impacted back to its original position. Usually some combination of the two occurs. It is during these periods of restoring harmony that people often experience feelings of confusion and dislocation. It is also why we don't experience growth in a smooth and orderly manner. Moreover as Carana explained to you earlier using the analogy of the muscles, we can't continually stretch out. Each stretch must be followed by a rest, and sometimes a contraction, as every cell in the body adjusts to the new position. And since no cell exists in isolation, but rather in relationship to every other cell in the body, then it follows naturally that the adjustment process must proceed until all cells have adjusted to each other. At that point the whole organism achieves with balance and harmony a new and higher level of functioning.'

"I wasn't sure if I completely understood all of Ardana's explanation, but she assured me not to worry about understanding everything completely the first time. She said it was necessary for everybody to return to their same lessons and also to approach them in different ways. Each approach impacted differently on the body until the lesson became an integral part of their consciousness.

"'We all owe a measure of gratitude to you and Adonara for your part on the mountaintop during our ritual to contact the great goddess. You know now from Carana's explanation about the circumstances leading to your separation from our group at that time. In his teachings of rebirths he informed you of the learning process that results not only throughout a lifetime from birth to death, but also from the transitional states of being born, dying, and the period following death until moving into another rebirth. One major lesson that everyone needs to learn and you still needed to perfect coming into this lifetime is forgiveness.'

"I began to experience some discomfort as Ardana discussed forgiveness. I felt I already had some understanding of this—or at least I was aware of it—and, while I had consciously worked on it, I knew there were some areas in which I still needed to make more progress. The mere mention of it, though, was like a dull jab in my side; an unwelcome reminder of something I could no longer ignore.

"This involved a situation that began several years ago. It concerned a married couple that a colleague of mine wanted me to meet at a company function. He had mentioned them to me a few times, with the pretext that we were people that just had to meet, and for some reason that I could never quite fathom, was anxious we should meet. The intrigue and curiosity with which I naturally anticipated meeting them was mixed, however, with a vague anxiety, the source of which I couldn't discern. I decided my feelings were just the nervousness one experiences in anticipation of meeting new people with the hope of making a good impression. Yet as I approached both the time and the place of our appointed rendezvous, an unfamiliar foreboding completely overtook my emotions.

"I arrived before they did at this reception, and before most others had arrived; a fact that meant my energy, after scrutinizing those already present in the room, was consumed with examining every newcomer. My search was not only for the comfort and security that I hoped seeing my colleague would provide, but also, and probably more dominantly, in the even greater hope that just meeting this couple might relieve the dread that tugged at my heart with a fist of anger and resentment. As a result of my besieged behavior, everyone walking in who was not the prize became instead another assistant of the torturer.

"The prize, however, is generally bestowed. When they finally did arrive, I was rewarded in the most devastating way. The feeling was immediate, and I'm sure I didn't hide it to anybody who reads energy. I literally felt crushed!… I had to get quickly away and find a sofa to sit down. I remember it really had to be a sofa, because I needed to sink deep down into it. I can't imagine what my colleague must have thought, but at the time that concern weighed little against the force compelling me out of there.

"I did not stay long on the sofa in that condition, when someone I thought I recognized rushed to my side, and, seeing how my energy had just drained out of me, helped me out the door to get some fresh air. I remarked that I was already feeling much better when he asked how I was doing, and then suggested I go directly home. When I turned around to thank him, he had totally vanished. Yet I still felt his hand on my shoulder.

"I have no idea how long it took me to play back this memory sequence, but all of a sudden it occurred to me that Ardana had been talking to me. I looked at her with that expression of surprise one often has when popping out of a daydream, and she was looking at me with the most placid expression of love, patience, and compassion I had ever felt, as though the very goddess herself were holding me in her vision. I didn't want to interrupt her discussion about forgiveness, but I was seized with the need to have another question answered first.

"'Ardana, what did Carana mean when he said that as the existence of my soul just continued, you've been in constant contact with us?'

"'Well, it is true we've all had contact with you during your unincarnated states as well as your incarnated ones. But it's also true that you have visited us. I don't know how well you remember that time, but it was a real treat, especially because it meant you were trying to find your way back to us.' Looking more baffled than ever, Ardana encouraged me to remember: 'It was many years ago when you were still in college. You were listening to a recording of music typical to our region, when suddenly you found yourself amongst us.'

"Immediately an intense energy swept over me as I recalled the incident she described. I was indeed listening to a recording of the flute and harp music typical of the people in the Andean region of South America. All of a sudden I experienced the strangest shift in energy that had ever happened to me. I found myself sitting in a circle of musicians playing the music I had been listening to. It was on top of a mountain high in the Andes, and I felt the sharp and crisp mountain air as it whisked against my face and hair. As I stayed there, a surge of energy started to sweep through me as it traveled around from person to person, over and over again. Finally, overcome with the intensity of the energy, I found myself back in my physical body in my room at school.

"The look of amazement that played across my face indicated my surprise at that meeting. At the time I was merely struck at the intense and unusual nature of the experience but wasn't able to bring back into my conscious awareness the knowledge of whom I had visited. My thoughts were more focused on what might have caused such a totally new event. I asked Ardana what brought it about.

"'Again, Narada, it comes back to the issue of energy and sensitivity. Everything that exists vibrates at a certain frequency. It is the particular frequency of every object that gives it the unique set of properties we observe with our five senses. What really happens is our senses allow us to resonate with those unique properties. This is why different people will perceive the same object differently. Because people have different levels of sensitivity in each of their senses, they resonate differently toward the same object. We all know people who have more acute seeing; some have more sensitive noses; some hear things others don't. Such varying levels of sensitivity may change in response to temporary physical ailments, and momentary moods. You know, for example, how anger can block perception. When you're in a rage, you just won't perceive things that are quite clear when you're relaxed. If you have a cold, you may not detect the delectable aromas of certain foods, or they may even smell bad.

"'It is not only with our five physical senses, however, that we perceive things. We also have emotional responses to actions and events. What we are really doing is responding to the energetic vibration of the event. How do you observe love, for example? Can you see, smell, taste, hear, or touch it? You can't, but you still feel it, or, more accurately, you resonate with it; resonate with the vibration of love that someone else is communicating to you. And just like our physical senses, we all have different levels of sensitivity to perceiving emotions; meaning we may all perceive the same emotion differently. And, moreover, there are circumstances that also temporarily alter these perceptions. If we're very depressed, for instance, we may not appreciate, or even recognize, the love and concern others may be showing us. Our ability to respond to someone else's emotion—that is, resonate with it—depends on the emotion we happen to be vibrating to at the time. It's obvious that we respond very differently to someone else's anger when we are also very angry, as opposed to when we're feeling very loving.

"'Now, why does it seem that some people, more than others, are able to reach out further to other people, to connect with them more deeply, empathize more intensely with their emotional states? Just as we perceive objects through our physical senses, and react to emotions through our emotional senses, there are even more subtle aspects to our being that allow us to connect and identify with others. This may be described by some as the level of our spiritual development. At the extremes, we have people who can't tell the difference between another human being and a rock, to those who identify strongly with all other people, and, indeed, with all other animate and inanimate life forms. They have this ability because they have become aware of the life force that sustains them, and they know that the very same life force sustains other forms as well. Therefore, when they consciously resonate with the life force, they resonate with everything else in existence.

"'Because we all have varying levels of sensitivity in all areas of our being, each one of us perceives different things. As some people will see, hear, or smell something on the physical plane that is totally imperceptible to others, there are some people who can perceive and have experiences on the non-physical planes that are just not available to others. There is nothing mystical or magical about this; it's just a matter of individual development. It is built into the essential makeup of all individuals. We are hot-wired for it, if you will. It is integral to the reason we are sustained through multiple lives: that each time we develop more of our innate potential, and become more sensitive on the physical, emotional, and spiritual levels, until we develop through divine, cosmic and unity consciousness and become masters of energy and energetic manipulation.

"'What you think was a totally new event for you, Narada, when you left your body and visited with us, actually came about because of other experiences you had that year that prepared you for the event.' Once again, I was clueless and had to have my memory jogged. 'Try to recall two other events in which you left your body, prior to your soul visit to us.'

"I remembered these two events immediately, and wondered if Ardana were doing something to facilitate my memory. The first one was quite vivid, effortless, and unexpected. I was indeed at school and it happened in my room in the dormitory. I was at my desk studying, and, perhaps unwisely, had the radio on, which did more to distract than assist me. A piece of music came on that I found so exquisitely beautiful that it focused my attention away from my book. I became aware of an energy coalescing in my gut and moving up through my body as the music—a long orchestral introduction to a piano concerto—continued to play. As soon as the piano itself started, the energy that had been moving upward, shot out the top of my head. All of a sudden I realized I was floating near the ceiling. I looked down and saw that my body was still at my desk, but my consciousness and seat of my perceptions was outside of it.

"The second experience occurred shortly afterwards. It was late in the evening and I was walking through the campus, which was mostly deserted and quiet at that time. I began to focus on the movement of my walking, whose rhythm seemed to mesmerize me. Once again, the formation and flow of energy, like the time before, sent my conscious awareness out of body. I looked down and saw my body walking, but the part I identified with was floating above and observing the physical part.

"I was still engaged in the pleasant memory of those events when Ardana spoke again. 'You probably cannot recall most of the times we visited you, Narada, can you?' I was dumbfounded by her question, as I never even contemplated such a time. Once again, Ardana jogged my memory. 'Let me remind you first of something Carana told you yesterday. His explanation will help ease your anxiety about not being able to recall certain events. He said that when an individual experiences something new for which no file or category previously exists, the new impression may just be dumped into a pre-existing file with associations totally inappropriate to it. Do you remember that?'

"Ardana maintained her loving manner toward me. No tone of impatience or reprimand could ever be found at all in her voice. Nothing I could say or do would appear foolish to her, as some energy that constantly emanated from her embraced me with a totally unconditional love.

"'Most times our visits occurred on the psychic plane, usually while you slept. One visit which incurred a physical materialization happened during an incident you just recalled yourself when I began to discuss forgiveness.'

"*Oh Lord*, I thought to myself with some alarm, *I feel as though I'm being tested*! There were so many new thoughts and old memories swimming around my head at that moment, I didn't quite know which one she was referring to and which one I was supposed to select. She read my panic and came to my rescue by reminding me about the incident regarding the couple my colleague introduced me to. All of a sudden I remembered that throughout my trip back home after the reception, the mystery of the stranger who helped me dominated my thoughts and emotions and overshadowed my reaction to meeting that couple. The event was so baffling that before I went to bed that night I figured either I must have imagined it due to the trauma I had just experienced, or, more likely, the person from the reception who helped me out rushed back inside long before I turned around, and I just continued to feel the pressure from his hand on my shoulder. When I woke up the next morning the only thought I gave it was how I managed the long drive home in my condition, as I was so distracted I couldn't remember paying any attention to the road or my driving.

"'Are you telling me, Ardana, that the person who helped me was one of you?' A broad smile played across her face, and in it an expression that revealed she had been looking forward to sharing the memory of this event with me.

"'Indeed, Narada, that was I who came to your assistance.' On the canvas of my surprised countenance Ardana completed the painting of that scene. 'Knowing who that couple was, and aware that your encounter with them was inevitable, I remained on the look out. I knew it would probably have a devastating affect on you, and I wanted to be there to help you through it. It was essential to get you out of that environment as quickly as possible because the result of that encounter could have seriously and negatively impacted your health. When you thought I vanished, all I did was dematerialize, but I stayed with you until you got home. In fact I guided your driving home. If I had let you drive alone you would have wrapped yourself around a tree; such was the state you were in.

"'Let us end this discussion for the day, Narada, because I can tell you need some time to absorb all that we've talked about today. You've been sufficiently stretched out for the time being. In fact, why don't you take the rest of the day and do some physical stretching and exercises. Tomorrow we can resume our discussion on forgiveness.'

"I was very glad myself to stop where we did. My head was a jumbled mess at that point, and while I had numerous questions to ask of Ardana, I could formulate none of them. Like a funnel clogged with too much stuff too quickly, it would take some time for all my thoughts and emotions to settle down before I could utter an articulation of any of them. I took the advice she left me with and found relief from stretching my limbs and torso. I followed this with a brisk walk through an adjacent wooded area and soon felt vibrant and alert. That evening Ardana and the others complimented me on my condition and teased me by suggesting how good the mountain air was for my complexion. I certainly felt wonderful; kind of like acing a test after studying really hard, then outdoing your best record on the track. I already felt myself performing at a higher level of functioning and was charged with the desire to attain more. I was affected by my closeness to Ardana and looked forward to being with her the next day.

"After my morning ritual and a light breakfast with Ardana, she resumed her discussion on forgiveness. 'The inability to forgive is a major obstacle on the path of spiritual advancement, Narada. It is a great challenge for all human beings. There is a particular level on the path that cannot be attained until forgiveness has been mastered. You may not yet recall how we all had been working intensely in this area. Our final test, if you will, came with the blast that tore the mountain asunder and physically ripped you and Adonara from us. We were able to work together to move beyond while it remained an active lesson for you. Now it is your turn.

"'It is through complete forgiveness that we are able to move beyond the limitations of the physical plane. Forgiveness is letting go. More accurately, it is seeing with divine perception that enables you to let go. What is it we have to let go?; the question I see dancing in your eyes! People are strongly tied to the seemingly infinite wrongs of which they perceive themselves the victims. When you believe someone has done something bad to you, has hurt you in some way, you feel unjustly wronged. So, the typical response—which is supported by everyone as proper action—is to defend your honor, vindicate the rightness of your position, and retaliate. Such noble sentiments and actions only enslave you further. What could be used in a positive manner to advance your spiritual awareness becomes instead a lead weight tied around the leg you're using to reach the mountaintop.

"'This is action governed by human perception, not divine. Humans are severely limited by perceiving only with their five physical senses. These senses communicate to them only the superficial differences among people. Such limited information makes them conclude that each individual is a separate entity with its own unique boundaries. When people react to the actions they perceive wronged them, they reinforce their notion of themselves as a limited, isolated, self-contained, and separate physical being. Their belief that they have been wronged constitutes a strong mental thought. As with all thoughts this sends out a vibration to the person's whole body. The vibration is strong because it is charged with a strong emotional feeling. Every physical cell in that body receives the communication of that vibration, and as the vibration is one of anger, discord, and separation, every cell then takes on those qualities.

"'People become so justified in their feelings of how they've been wronged that they continue to reinforce those vibrations. This is very common and also easy to observe. You have probably already done so. Try and recall how someone's body will completely change by a mere thought. Perhaps that person heard a name or saw someone's resemblance in a picture or in somebody else. Instantly the body cringes and contorts, and the person communicates a totally different energy. The person may even no longer remember the initial wrong, but the body does. It is now firmly locked into that vibration. For most people this phenomenon occurs as the result of not just one wrong incident, but rather from many. If they could only remember them all, people would be able to create a long list of bad things that others did to them, or good things they didn't. The unfortunate result of such behavior prevents people from breaking through their barriers of separation, and attaining extraordinary freedom.

"'People cannot master forgiveness, however, if they are still tied to judgment. Most of the actions by which people feel injured are things that never even affect them directly, but rather, are actions that violate their sense of values or moral principles. As people develop into adulthood, the identity they form of themselves is constituted by a whole set of ideas about the way they and others should behave, think, and feel. This is to some extent a generalization, as everyone holds to a different set and range of behaviors, thoughts and feelings they believe permissible for themselves and others. Nevertheless, the dynamic is similar.

When someone displays a behavior, thought, or feeling that falls outside that set and range, he can react with an indignation as though he were personally violated.

"'Even if people strongly believe in the need and rightness of their values and principles, their sense of judgment extends beyond that. It's amazing how many people react with judgment to the minor differences found in others. They react in disgust to someone who is too fat, too skinny, too short, or too tall. They're indignant if someone appears too unkempt, too prim and proper, too jovial, or too depressed. They're put off by those who don't work much or those who work too hard. They dislike those who are better looking, wealthier, and more successful, and look down on those who are poor and beaten down. They pass judgment on people based on their gender, skin color, religion, ethnic group, sexual orientation, language accent, and level of intelligence. The specific dislikes and level of intensity differ from person to person, but most people, if they examine their thoughts closely enough, will likely find their particular ones.

"'Most people are probably unaware of the extent of their judgments. If they were, and kept a list, they would be amazed how long it would be. Many of these same people may also not care that they hold judgments and even feel it's good to have them. That's certainly for each person to decide. The important thing to know for everyone who is consciously on the path toward spiritual awareness is that judgmental behavior retards their growth and prevents them from attaining true freedom and liberation.

"'Judgment also involves obsessive and possessive behavior. When we judge something or someone, we may have a strong desire to see things our own particular way. Many people will object to this characterization as too strong, but that may be because they haven't tried to give up judging others. When we are possessive about a person or object it's obvious we can't let it go. In judgment, we seek to possess others in our own particular image; expect them to be the way we think is right or proper. We obsess over thoughts that keep us locked into certain emotional states. Examples of such thoughts might be: *I don't know why so-and-so doesn't like me; Why doesn't she call me; How come he got promoted and I didn't; I'm always so tired I just can't do it; I just can't remember a thing; I just can't get anything right; What's wrong with him—can't seem to get anything right; Wow, look at all those scars on his body—there must be something terribly wrong with him*. Or we meet someone and wonder how developing an acquaintance or friendship will help further our own ambitions. Even when our attachment to someone or something comes from a deep love, and we want to possess them and believe we can't live without them, we still retard our spiritual growth.

"'Whether from holding on to the indignation of being wronged, from a sense of judgment, or from an appetite for possessiveness, people will be limited in their spiritual growth. When our perception is based on physical senses we remain bound to the physical plane of existence, regardless of whether our perception results in a strong rejection or loving attachment. When we derive our understanding of ourselves—our identity— from a socially accepted construct of the way things should be, then we must proceed through life with the limitations which that construct naturally imposes on people.

"'Letting go of all these limitations is ultimately what forgiveness is all about. But it is a process more than a single act. One doesn't just let something go as simply as letting an object fall through one's fingers. On the contrary, each forgiveness involves a transformation of our energetic configuration. I said earlier that everything that exists vibrates at a certain frequency. Yet this is true not only of objects, but of thoughts and feelings as well, because it is through our thoughts and feelings that we are able to connect with other people and other objects. To put it a different way, we develop relationships with others through the connections of our thoughts and feelings. Through our thoughts the connection is established on the mental level. The level of our emotions involved with that particular thought determines the strength of the connection. That connection establishes the relationship between person and object or between two people. In a relationship, the other person or object is brought into your psychic space, and you become transformed in the process. That is because you now bring the vibration of that person or object into your energy field. More precisely, you bring into your field the energy formed of your own *perception* of the other person or object. In other words, when you don't see the essential or intrinsic nature of the other, you wrap it up in the energy of your own attraction and desire, or repulsion and disgust, then resonate with the energy the way you have so qualified it.

"'The world around us with everything in it is like our mirror. Everything inside ourselves is reflected back to us. Unfortunately we are very selective in the way we use the mirror. We only hold it up to those things we want to see reflected back, and with those reflected things we don't like we blame the mirror. That is, when we see someone acting in a way that really disturbs us, it is more common to wonder what is wrong with him and blame him for his aggravating behavior. Our orientation in this situation tells us: *There's nothing wrong with me; I'm perfectly normal, but this guy is really off his rocker.* Instead of seeing something of ourselves reflected in this other person, we project our judgments and limitations.

"'True letting go, therefore, must involve establishing a new relationship with the other that transcends attraction or repulsion. It requires seeing the other not as you might want it to be, or as you judge it to be, but as it truly is. It is seeing the other not from the role of the victim, nor from the role of the weak, nor the strong, the self-righteous or indignant, nor the wounded or the victor, but rather with all your masks and filters removed. It means seeing the other not from some social construct of regulations and limitations imposed on you as a consequence of your membership in some society or group, but instead with a pure mind and heart. It means knowing that the other may be your mirror and having the courage to acknowledge that if something is being reflected back that really disturbs you, then it is a great opportunity to look inside your own self. When you do so, you may discover that what really disturbs you about this other person exists within yourself as well. Since you do not want to admit you may be like this, or that you may also have this element, then it becomes easier to fault the mirror—the person reflecting it back.

"'Just the awareness of the way others serve as our mirror can be beneficial, however. When we understand the dynamic of something, we have a choice in our behavior. Without awareness we react automatically and mechanically, like robots. When we know how we operate, we can decide consciously how we wish our behavior to be; how we wish to respond. Thus, when we understand these things, instead of being at the mercy of some encounter, we can actually use them for our ultimate benefit. This empowers us in a way to which others respond, although not in the way they're expecting.'

"'Ardana,' I asked, 'in what way can people actually use this understanding for their own benefit?'

"'Well, for example, let's take two people, called Mary and John. Say Mary behaves in a way that disturbs John. He can then respond in two different ways: from a habitual, gut-level reaction or from higher awareness. In the first way, John gets tense and knotted up inside, becomes indignant and starts to boil. John feels insulted and lashes out to defend what he feels is the rightness of his position or simply to demonstrate that someone else just can't offend him and get away with it! So he lashes out at Mary, and the situation escalates as she counter-reacts the same as John.

"'John can respond to Mary another way, however, because he understands how energy works. When Mary's behavior bothers him, he realizes that she has served as his mirror to reflect something in him that he doesn't like and probably didn't even realize existed. In his mind and heart, John thanks Mary for being there for him in order to help him realize something about himself. Mary, of course, is most likely totally unaware of the role she played, because she doesn't understand John and what he still has to work out in his life. Moreover she is most likely expecting— and hoping—that her behavior will provoke John to some outrage. She is all set for a counter strike, but John never provides the opportunity.

"'In his simple act of awareness, John has accomplished two things. The first is that he saw something in himself that he hadn't realized existed, that it didn't please him, and that now he could work on eliminating or transforming it. The second thing he accomplished was to stop immediately the interaction with Mary from becoming more stressful and bitter, which would have made future interactions between them even more difficult. Now he maintains an open channel with her so they can continue to work productively together.

"'Let me pause for a moment, Narada, and let you unburden your anxious mind of its questions.' I had indeed formulated questions as Ardana spoke, and hoped I'd be able to remember them all. I first asked what she meant by saying it is seeing with divine perception that enables you to let go.

"'Most people's acknowledged perception comes from their five physical senses. Most of what they observe with these senses can then be appropriately categorized and catalogued. And the general consensus concerning their observations reinforces the validity of those senses. For example, you observe an object and see that it has a particular color, and feel it has a certain texture and weight; it has some odor, tastes bitter, and makes no sound. Everyone else observing that object makes the same observations. You come to a consensus regarding the nature of that object, and therefore, have no need to believe the object is anything else, or more, than that. Because you observe the physical properties of that object, you conclude it is a unique entity that exists in isolation and separate from all other objects, including yourself. It is the most natural conclusion, everyone accepts it, and most people believe it is absurd to challenge it. Scientific instruments can measure very accurately all the properties you have observed with your senses, further confirming your observations and beliefs.

"'Seeing with divine perception is different. And I use the word *divine* not in any religious sense, but rather to distinguish it from the average person's normal mode of observation, as I just described it. It's divine in the way that it transcends the physical properties and boundaries perceived by the physical senses. You see, an object may be described as having certain qualities, but what is the origin of these properties? Well, you answer, they derive from the molecular structure unique to that object. The physical molecules, however, as well as their even smaller physical components, maintain their unique relationship among themselves as a result of their symbiotic vibrations. The essence of those vibrations is divine, pure, or cosmic intelligence. It is this ultimate intelligence from which everything we perceive is manifested. Therefore, when we perceive with divine perception we can look past the physical properties that seem to separate objects through their differences, and allow ourselves to resonate with the object. In the same way the basic elements of the object vibrate within their symbiotic relationship, so are we, and in fact all objects and people integrally enmeshed within the same web of divine intelligence. This is the basis, as you'll learn later, for creating much of the extraordinary phenomena you have observed around here.'

"'In your example of John and Mary,' I asked Ardana, 'was it this perception that motivated John's behavior?'

"'Well, that's a good question, Narada, but as with much of the material we're discussing, is not simply answered. While total awareness allows us to behave that way, how do we get there? Much of our growth stems from a dynamic ratcheting process, back and forth between performing things from the old, habitual way, and experimenting with a new way. If the new way achieves different results which also prove beneficial, then we are inclined to repeat it. The individual is no longer a slave to his habitual behaviors or thought patterns, but can now allow him- or herself to operate from a position of greater awareness. This awareness, having now become an integral part of his vibrational make-up, remains as a reminder the next time a similar situation arises. He then has the option of how to proceed, and the outcome will further reinforce the validity of his new awareness. In my example of John and Mary, John was experimenting with that notion of seeing Mary as a mirror to his own inner issues, and whether behaving differently would change the outcome, which previously had always been one of degenerating confrontations with Mary.

"'The successful outcome of John's alternate approach to dealing with Mary reinforces his ability to perceive differently. He has begun to notice the difference between feeling separate from others due to his observations of physical properties, and the deep connection with others he experiences when he sees with his divine perception.'

"'Ardana, is that what you meant by pure mind and heart?' 'Exactly,' she replied. 'Normal perception sees through the mental window that is covered with innumerable and conditioned thoughts regarding the nature of things and through the heart window that is covered with innumerable feelings of desire and repulsion. Such windows distort true perception to the extent they are cloudy and covered up. With pure mind and heart, the windows have been removed, and the individual can now look past the clouded windows of others and observe their own pure minds and hearts. When those with clouded windows look at the one whose windows have been removed, they may find something very different reflected back to them. What is reflected back is their own essential purity. However, depending on how cloudy they are they may or may not perceive their own essential purity. This is why many people never recognized the advanced masters like Christ and Buddha who walked among them nor the advanced masters who walk in their midst today. Their windows are so covered up with the thoughts and feelings of separation and isolation that no light can penetrate to their core. This is why those who have begun to clean up their windows to allow some light to penetrate experience an exquisite delight in the presence of a master. The pure light from the master penetrates their windows and sets up a symbiotic vibration within their own essence until their whole being resonates with that vibration.'

"Ardana sensed I was beginning to lose my focus and was inclined to quit for the day. While it's true that I felt I needed time to absorb and understand everything she had been discussing, I still had two burning questions based on things she had said earlier. The first came from her account of the evening at the reception when my colleague introduced me to that couple. She said that she came to my rescue immediately and escorted me outside. 'Ardana,' I said, 'you told me you came to my aid at the reception, but that person was a man!'

"'Narada, you understand now the difference between ordinary and divine perception, so you can figure out how you observed me then. You might say that you lost your divine sight at that moment due to the shock you had received. You were weakened and only had sufficient energy to engage your physical perception. Nevertheless it still registered in you that there was something familiar about me. Because of your fragile state, I had to appear in a way that would not shock you further and would seem as the most normal thing for someone there to assist you. The form I assumed allowed me to blend in with the surroundings and the company, and arouse the least suspicions and sense of impropriety from the other guests. If your divine sight had been completely open then, you would have seen that my form was just a materialization and substantively different from the others. Now, I believe, there was still another issue troubling you?'

"'You said earlier that now it was my turn. What exactly did you mean by that?'

"'Oh, my dear Narada, your question is right on target! There is an extraordinary and complex web of relationships among people throughout the world. It connects people in the most unlikely ways and from the most unexpected and diverse regions. The web consists of energetic connections and is formed through the thoughts, feelings, and events that one individual directs toward, or establishes with, another individual. These thoughts, feelings, and events link the psychic or non-material aspect of the human being. As a consequence, these connections may remain despite the demise of the physical body. Two people, for example, strongly united in the bond of love, maintain that connection after their deaths. They may subsequently reincarnate in different countries, and even as different sexes, but the connection remains.

How it is then played out, of course, depends on numerous other circumstances. In another example, two people may be strongly united because one killed the other. Again how that is subsequently played out may vary. Nevertheless these links remain vital and interactive until canceled.'

"'How are they canceled, 'I asked,' and what happens if they're not canceled?

"'Through what we have been discussing today: forgiveness! But only true forgiveness, which comes deep from the heart and soul of the person, has sufficient force to release the energy bound up in the originally created connection. If they're not canceled they remain, and one after the other, increasingly bind the person in an entangled mess of connections. How far can a caged bird fly? How far can a man walk with his feet tied together? Attaining spiritual freedom and liberation requires removing the psychic shackles that bind our minds and hearts.'

"'But surely,' I protested, 'bonds of love can't be restricting!'

"'Yes, even bonds of love. At least the way many people have created them. Most bonds of love, even the most intense—in fact, most probably among the most intense—may have within them strong elements of attraction, desire, co-dependency, and fear. People depend on their partners to provide things from comfort and security to performing certain chores. They fear losing their partners, being alone, and providing for themselves all those things formerly done by their partners. So it is these attachments of love that people must let go because they ultimately ensnare and prevent them from expressing true and unconditional love.

"'Regarding being your turn, when I said that, you may remember, I also said that our final test came with the blast that tore the mountain asunder and physically ripped you and Adonara from us. I mentioned that we had all been working intensely on forgiveness, including you. Naturally, as a result of that blast, powerful connections were created between each one of us and those responsible for it. Our final test of forgiveness, therefore, entailed dissolving those connections so we could be free to move on. It was truly a test, because, as you know, we were not only very fond of you and Adonara, but there was also a strong bond among all of us.

"'So now you probably understand what I meant by your turn. It is even more difficult for you and Adonara, because as it was you who were ripped not only from our group but also from your bodies, the connection that was created between you and the killers is very strong.'

"'How can I do that?' I asked Ardana, faintly betraying a veiled fear and anxiety. 'I don't even know who they are or how to find them!'

"'First of all, Narada, you do know who they are, although you may not consciously want to admit it. Secondly, you also know how to find them. Unfortunately we can't help you with this one. Figuring it out is part of the lesson.

"'Why don't you take the remainder of the day alone, Narada, to rest and contemplate what I've talked about today. I can see the energy has closed in around you, allowing nothing else to penetrate. And don't knock yourself out in the process. You'll have other opportunities to return to these lessons, and the rest of us will have their own ways of teaching.'

"Ardana then walked away and left me alone. I was also tired of staying in the same place, so I decided to go for a walk as a way to distract myself. I got up and headed toward a wooded area I hadn't yet explored. I felt heavy as I walked, as though I were dragging a weight behind me. My head felt so stuffed I couldn't think anymore, yet after a while I realized that I had been repeating unconsciously some of Ardana's last words in my mind, almost like a mantra: 'You know who they are and you know how to find them. You know who they are and you know how to find them.' Over and over. It seemed as if my walking became lighter and that some natural rhythm was established between my gait and my mantra. I was too mentally fatigued to analyze these patterns and felt content to suspend any thought process and be carried by the rhythm.

"After a while I found myself in a place both strange and familiar. I had reached the summit of some peak, a beautiful spot that commanded distant views in all directions. Though surrounded by woods, the area on top was a lush meadow, and except for one corner, appeared to form a perfect circle. The deformed section attracted my curiosity, but as I approached it, an unsettling foreboding covered me like a shroud. The unusual mountain scar seemed created by a slide in the terrain. Like the repulsion of vertigo one experiences while perched over the balcony of a high-rise that sends him scurrying back into the apartment, I quickly sought refuge in the center of the meadow. Although I felt both agitated and relieved, these feelings had a new and unrecognizable quality about them.

With nothing to shield it, the sun bathed the meadow in its warmth. I opened myself up to its comforting embrace with the hope that it might soothe away the agitation like some healing ointment on an open wound. I soon felt like a child cradled in the secure arms of his mother rocking him to sleep.

"I must have dozed off because afterwards I realized I had experienced a bizarre and terrifying dream. In the dream I was still on the mountaintop, no longer alone, but in the company of my spiritual family. I experienced the mortifying blast that Carana and Ardana had recounted—in which they always ended their story. This time, however, I was aware of being instantly yanked out of my body and witnessing like an outside observer both the reactions of my family and the tumbling of my body. I followed it to the base of the mountain and saw it crushed under tons of rubble. My attention was then immediately diverted some small distance away by the satanic cry of sinister laughter. Following it into the inner sanctuary of the local church I witnessed the top two priests of the religious hierarchy alternately doubled over in merriment and strutting around like puffed-up peacocks. Seeing my family in shock and despair, I vowed to move earth itself to avenge them.

"Yelling at them with a piercing anger, I startled myself out of my dream. I looked around self-consciously to determine if I needed to handle any embarrassment but as before found the meadow my only company. I headed back with the approaching dusk and the hope I could find my way. My hope never became fear, however, and I walked with an assurance born of familiarity. When I arrived at the temple, everyone was there just awaiting my appearance. While delighted to see me, they also seemed to express a searching inquiry regarding my well-being, as though I had gone through some trauma. Nothing was said on that score, however, and we all enjoyed another evening of fun and merriment."

Chapter Four

Moving Energy

“Iwas expecting to see someone besides Ardana the next day, and sure enough, when I arrived at the temple, Jandara was there waiting for me. What I was not expecting, however, was the way she greeted me: 'Narada, get your lazy-ass bones over here and eat so we can get on with your damn lessons!' Her voice was harsh and attacking, so unlike anything I had experienced since I arrived at the mountaintop, and left me stunned. The brisk pace that brought me to the temple that morning turned into a stagger as I felt my legs go limp. It seemed as though my energy and vitality just drained right out of me. Mentally I became befuddled and found I couldn't even mutter a coherent reply. I remained dumbfounded and wondered if I had done something to offend her. I staggered over to the food table across from her, but my appetite had vanished. I turned away from her to look at something more familiar and comforting, when suddenly I sensed someone right behind me. I had no time to turn around before I felt that person's arms around me.

"'I'm sorry, Narada, for greeting you this way, but I needed to show you something, and this was the most effective way. Please forgive me.'

"I quickly turned around. Jandara looked completely different. In place of the stern, rigid face that had earlier greeted me was a soft and lovely countenance, whose radiant smile framed her sparkling eyes. I found her warm and loving embrace healing, and soon felt my strength, and appetite, returning. 'Come and let's eat something,' she suggested, 'then I'll explain what this was all about.' While my appetite had certainly returned, I felt I ate more than I wanted to, perhaps from a lingering anxiety that the earlier mixed messages were not yet over. When she did resume her discussion, however, she assured me that her approach would only work the first time with me.

"'Narada, tell me how you were feeling when you came to the temple this morning before I spoke, how you felt after my greeting, and how you changed again.'

"'Well,' I said, 'at first I was feeling really upbeat. Then when you spoke to me, I felt as though someone had punched me in the stomach. I lost my appetite, as well as the enthusiasm and vigor I had when I arrived. Of course I began to feel much better after you embraced me, though I must admit I still had some lingering anxiety.'

"'Well, I'm certainly glad you're feeling better. I'd like you now to close your eyes, get comfortable, and take a few deep breaths. Turn your attention away from me and focus inside yourself. Examine those places where you felt anxiety and loss of vitality, and see how they feel now.' I told her all the anxiety had dissipated, that I felt tranquil, and was enjoying our interaction. 'Now, remember this morning's events, but instead of telling me as you just did how you felt, this time I want you actually to capture those feelings, feel them again, and tell me immediately about them.'

"I did the exercise as she directed me and experienced with almost the same intensity my reaction to how she first spoke to me. I tried to tell her about it, but once again felt an uncomfortable anxiety in my stomach and felt my energy draining away. I seemed to lack the will to say more and remained quiet.

"'Did you notice, Narada, the difference between recalling your experience mentally as opposed to recalling it emotionally? When you first thought about it you were able to tell me how you felt, and as you spoke you felt strong and confident. In other words, your recounting did not match the feelings you were describing. The second time you actually relived the experience. Even your body language responded appropriately. I don't know if you observed how you began to bring up your knees, curl up your body, and fold your arms around yourself. You became dumbfounded and couldn't articulate how you were feeling. Do you see how we hide behind our intellect? We can protect ourselves from experiencing certain emotions by distancing ourselves from them intellectually. Unfortunately this also prevents us from harnessing the power of those emotions and using them for our own purposes, instead of being used by them, as is the case with most people.'

"'What do you mean by harnessing them?' I asked Jandara.

"'Let me explain that by going through some more exercises. Close your eyes as before, get comfortable, and take some deep breaths. Scan your body and see if you can observe any places of tension or anxiety. Allow those feelings to drain out of you with each exhalation. If you are not able to scan or you can't observe any stresses, then just allow yourself to accept that if you do happen to have them, you can let them go with each out-breath. Now recall emotionally how you felt that time at the reception to which your colleague invited you to meet his friends. Don't just think about it, but allow yourself to relive it, to experience again the emotions that accompanied that event.'

"I did what she suggested and felt a complete transformation throughout my body. Once again I experienced the sense of being crushed and having the energy completely drain out of me. My body went limp, and Jandara told me I turned pale.

"'Now see, Narada, how this experience was even more removed in time and space than when I earlier assaulted you, yet you still relived that moment. You reacted strongly to an event which had already occurred. And do you know why? Recall what Ardana discussed about forgiveness. The emotions centered around this particular event in your life stem from an experience you still haven't let go. As a result the emotions remain and continue to exert an influence on you. It's not too difficult to relive the event because the emotions associated with it are integrally connected to you. By allowing yourself to connect emotionally to them, you can experience those emotions as they were the first time. If you just allow yourself to recall the event intellectually, you distance yourself from experiencing those emotions and consequently prevent yourself from realizing how those emotions still influence you. In order for forgiveness to be truly effective, you must be able to connect with the emotions. If you are distant from them—as through merely intellectualizing them—then your forgiveness lacks the power to let it all truly go. This is why people often wind up having to deal with issues of which they thought they had already let go. They probably only let go of part of them because they were unable to connect with them totally, generally due to fear of having to confront the issues again, feeling as though they don't have the proper resources to connect with the issue, or enough support once they do.

"'Okay, now I want you to clear yourself again, in the same manner you did before with the breathing, scanning, observing, acknowledging, and letting go. After you feel relaxed and centered, I want you to bring into your consciousness the memory of an event that you really enjoyed and made you feel good.'

"I got the relaxation part down okay, but the memory event part seemed to take a while. I was sure there had been many great times in my life, but perhaps the desire to focus on just the right or best one blocked anything from coming in; perhaps I felt I needed a really powerful moment. Finally, when none of the great moments volunteered to step forward, a shy and quiet one slipped out of the shadows. It was simply a serene time at the beach. Yet just recalling it triggered a depth of well-being. Maybe it was the relaxed state I was in, but the original sensations became so real. It was the perfect combination of warmth and sun in which you feel that the very air has become inspired to comfort you; that the sun smiles on you with a special love; that the sea breezes over you a welcome refreshment; and the birds, overjoyed with your company, delight you in their sweet serenade. Everything seemed so perfect. I was far away in an enchanted island of peace when I heard the faint and distant cry of my name. As the call became louder, I wondered who else was there and had recognized me.

"'Narada, I'm sorry to pull you out of your reverie, but it sure is obvious you managed to recall an event you enjoyed. I think you can see, though, how you can alter the way you're feeling by using your conscious thought process to recall an event then allow your emotions to resonate with the quality of the energy that characterized that event.

"'Let's do this exercise again using different circumstances. I know that you have, as so many others, been engaged in difficult and frustrating affairs of the heart; times when the burning desire for your lover wasn't returned; when hopes of even the tiniest response could sustain your yearning; when your fervor consumed all other thoughts in the fire of your love. And finally the agony born of the realization that your passion was one-sided, that only you had been fueling its fire. Capture that time and relive it.'

"For me I had more than one time from which to chose, yet the dynamics of all of them were similar. Each involved the same obsessive longing, the waiting for some gesture, a message, anything that might sustain the hope that I was also desired. When the obvious one-sidedness broke through the wall of my denial, the rubble came crashing down on my heart. It was more than just a metaphor. The weight of sadness and dejection that pressed on my chest was real, and it spread throughout my body like water pouring into a boat. It wasn't just the relationship, or the desire for one, that sank, but everything else whose meaning was constructed into it. When the water began to emerge from the opened cracks and slipped down in tears, Jandara once again brought me back to the reality of our exercise.

"'Not a fun time, was it, Narada? What did you do to emerge out of it?'

"The question struck me as a revelation. There was actually something I could have done! The astonishment on my face communicated my ignorance and desire for Jandara's lesson.

"'It's really quite simple,' she responded. 'While you still feel the weight of sadness from the lost love episode you've recalled, visualize in your mind another person, probably someone you've never even met, for whom you have the same feelings of desire. And, of course, don't get hung up on thinking you really have to see it. Whether your images manifest as actual scenes or just thoughts is not critical. This time your imagined lover returns the intensity of your passion, and you think or imagine both of you expressing your shared desire in various scenarios. I can see your energy has completely changed. Tell me what you experienced.'

"I don't know what Jandara saw, but I certainly experienced a total change in my being. The weight of sadness and dejection was lifted from me. My despair became delight; my constricted heart expanded. I became lighter, yet charged and anxious to move forward.

"'Good, Narada. Now play with these two experiences. Alternate your focus from one to the other and watch how your energy changes throughout your body, moving up and down, expanding and contracting. You see how you can control your mood, and along with it, the energy you experience and project. With practice you can cut the marionette strings from which you are suspended and hang your emotions there instead. Then, according to the particular effect you're seeking, you can dangle the appropriate emotion. This shift is critical to your development. Most people spend their lives being yanked around by their emotions, which are reactions to events outside them. While they may not be able to control such events or their outcomes, they can control, or at least influence to some degree, their emotional responses.

"'When you called into consciousness various events from your past, you experienced not just one feeling but several. Moreover when you recalled one occasion, numerous others also came to your mind. As though these various events were linked, tapping into one brought you into contact with others. This is not merely coincident. Rather vibrations from emotions produced by a particular event will set in motion similar emotions from other events, thus linking them together. It is not unlike the phenomenon of a string from a musical instrument which begins to vibrate in response to either the same note, or a different octave of that note, that emanates from a different source.

"'As a person moves through life, all the things that happen to him just don't come and go. They remain associated with him through more complex weavings of links. A new event may induce emotional reactions that appear to others as completely out of proportion or out of character to the event. The person undergoing such an emotional response may not understand himself the nature or strength of his own reaction. That's because of the unique emotional associations created in that person's history. The emotional response does not necessarily enable the individual to recall the event that brought on the particular emotions. In many cases fear, as well as the inability to resolve or handle the full emotional load, prevent the person from completely recalling the event. The end result, however, is basically the same: Attached to his marionette strings, the individual performs his unique dance as directed and choreographed by other people and external events.

"'Now, because of the way events are linked by sympathetic resonance, you can direct and choreograph your own dance as you will. In other words, instead of passively reacting to events outside of your control, you decide on the emotions you wish to animate your being, or, to put it another way, the quality of the energy that enables you to move through life; emotions being energy that has been qualified with a particular character. You have just done this. You have created a dramatic example of moving your energy from a negative, sluggish, and downward direction to one that was positive, strong, upbeat, life-enhancing, and life-promoting. You changed the quality of your energy from one that left you a hapless victim to one that put you in charge, in which you controlled the puppet strings.

"'The ability to do this is more important than just being able to turn your mood around. Because of the property of sympathetic resonance which I've discussed, the particular quality of energy that vibrates in your being attracts other events in your life with similar character. Moreover your energy will also attract similarly qualified energy from other sources. You had a good example of this many years ago when you were living with your partner in the city; do you remember?'

"I had no idea what Jandara was talking about and had to have my memory jogged. How these people could remember such things, much less even know about them, still mystified me. Nevertheless she was referring to a time when a planned trip outside our apartment that would have combined a pleasure walk with doing a task was preceded by an argument. What I had looked forward to with joy now turned into a drudge. My heart was no longer in it, and as we left the building I was seething and just felt like lashing out at somebody. Suddenly, just a few blocks away, someone out of nowhere jumped right in front of us and began to attack us when, curiously, his movements were arrested by some unseen force. We didn't stick around to investigate the cause of it but beat the hell out of there. Looking back I wondered if it were Jandara herself who halted that attack, which would explain why she knew about it. She responded to the quizzical expression on my face with a twinkle in her eyes.

"'Do you understand now why that guy attacked you, Narada? You were projecting such a strong energy of rage and lashing out that you attracted and essentially invited that mad man. This is not to say, of course, that people so easily bring on their own attacks, as most things in life are multi-causal, and also include karmic influences, which you will learn more about later. But it does mean that it helps to be aware of our moods, the quality of the energy we are feeling, and the propensity our energy has to attract other like-qualified energy. When we understand how this dynamic works, we can better protect ourselves. For instance, before you left your home that day, you and your partner could have stopped, done some conscious breathing together, and willfully altered your energy. In fact it helps to make this kind of exercise a regular practice. Because, as I mentioned earlier, people have created such a complex web of emotions and links in their psyche, much of it unconscious, they may be sending out unwanted emotional vibrations they're not even aware of. By learning to clear yourself, and willfully qualify your energy, you not only become more likely to attract what you want, but you also make it more difficult to pick up the emotional residue of those you pass. With sufficient and regular practice you become master of your energy and your moods.

"'A second, perhaps even more important reason for learning how to control your energy involves the ability to create your life, that is, to bring into it the events and circumstances you want. You've demonstrated for yourself that you can move your energy by focusing your attention, and that through vibrational resonance, you can attract other like energies to you. Logically, therefore, if you hold in your mind an idea or vision, you have the potential to bring that into your reality. Essentially you create it. Many people have now heard of this concept. Many of them have tried it and failed, thereby dismissing it as fantasy. The reason they have failed, however, has nothing to do with the concept, but rather, with how it is executed.

"'One obstacle people face in creating their reality is that they haven't become masters of controlling their energies and moods. Masters in any area, be it sports or the arts, become successful through regular practice, focus, single-mindedness, and resoluteness. Without such practice, people may desire something, then not focus sufficiently on it. Without single-mindedness, their attention wanders to other things, weakening the energy they're sending out. Sometimes these other things may contradict what they want. Without resoluteness they waver and doubt. This sends out energy that weakens the desired creation. Eventually their doubt becomes disbelief in the concept or in themselves. Either way the energy this communicates essentially cancels or alters the manifestation of their originally intended creation.

"'Another obstacle lies in the intended creation itself. That is, people often want things that are not in their own best interests. They're at cross purposes within themselves. While they may strongly and consciously desire something, unconsciously, or through the wisdom that filters down from their higher selves, an awareness of the imprudence of their desire counters their ability to create it. So, you see, our ability to manifest the creations of our desires also depends to some extent on being able to align our conscious desires with the wisdom of our higher selves and the purpose and direction of each of our lives. Not such an easy task.

"'Still, it would be unwise for people just to throw up their arms in frustration. While great accomplishments may not be easily attained, smaller ones are, and tend to move people onto a path that facilitates their growth and future attainment. That's because there's an accumulating affect. Each accomplishment, however small, attracts other people and other circumstances that enhance and propel the individual even further along. One trick that facilitates this process is to let go of the outcome. This may sound contradictory, but what often occurs is that becoming so fixated on the outcome sets people up for doubt and disappointment, and they give up their practice. If, instead, they make their practice the goal, then, before they realize it, their lives begin to change, their desires become manifested, and new people and things come to them—all of which further confirms the appropriateness and wisdom of their practice.'

"Jandara had more things to discuss with me, but felt I needed a break before moving on. Besides she said she got a call during our discussion from someone needing her assistance. I wasn't quite sure what she meant because I didn't see her with any beeper or cell phone, and even if she had an intuitive sense, the closest person would have required an absence longer than the time she allotted for our break. Still I was really happy to get a break and let my mind rest a while.

"I didn't feel like taking a walk, and was feeling comfortable where I was, so I decided just to stay and wait for Jandara. It was already late in the afternoon, and the warmth of the sun, having already seduced my laziness, now coaxed my eyes closed. The quiet and serenity of the place conspired to have me drift off and let the teachings go. Images rolled past my inner screen as though I were watching a silent movie. They were unfamiliar and sometimes strange. At one point scenes of a big city flicked by and I realized I was recognizing various stores, buildings, and other features. I moved through the streets like the ghost of a former resident. In my meanderings, I turned a corner onto a side street, and with tremendous surprise, saw, of all people, strolling down the sidewalk, myself and my former partner! I figured I had tapped into that scene because Jandara had reminded me of that period in my life. Still I wasn't sure if what I saw was just a mental construct of my dreaming mind or if I were back viewing an original event. Whatever it was, I longed for the film to continue to roll by as I was enjoying the sight of long-forgotten images.

"The figures of us were not especially pleasing to view, not because of any particular physical disfiguration, but rather due to a continuous display of unpleasant colors from which menacing objects burst forth. It was most peculiar, mainly because I couldn't remember ever seeing ourselves like that. It produced an unexpected and unsettling feeling in my stomach, which I found weird since I was disembodied. All of a sudden a frightful clash of colors and flying objects ensued as some violent man armed with a knife jumped in front of the pair with the intent to harm them. Before he could come down with his weapon, however, his arm was held fast, by none other than the figure of Jandara! As the two fled down the street, Jandara held him in a grip from which he couldn't escape, nor, strangely enough, seemed to want to escape. As she held him, his whole demeanor completely changed, and along with it, the palette of colors surrounding his body. From the dark and muddy cloud around him from which shot dark red daggers and arrows, he took on the colors of pink and blue. I called out to Jandara, but she didn't respond, and I figured she hadn't heard me. I repeated her name several times, louder and louder. Finally, along with the jabbing I felt in my arm, I heard her saying: 'I'm here, Narada, I'm here, wake up.' I opened my eyes, and Jandara was sitting next to me, with an amused look on her face.

"'Looks like you had an interesting trip. Maybe you can tell me about it some time. For now, however, I'd like to describe one more technique for moving and transforming the quality of your energy. Gratitude. It's simple, but practiced correctly, it can be very powerful.

"'Expressing gratitude enables us to make a positive connection with another individual, a group, or a higher power. Since the ultimate goal of our existence is to move from a consciousness centered in ego identity to unity- and cosmic-consciousness, then any positive and loving connection we can establish helps us toward that goal. In gratitude we open up our hearts and acknowledge the good that we have received from a source outside ourselves. This recognition helps move our energy toward our heart center—the heart chakra—and open it up, thus facilitating easier and stronger connections with others. Eventually we raise the energy higher, opening up deeper centers of insight and awareness. As these develop, the connections we establish become based on the resonance of increasingly more subtle energies. The vibrations of the most subtle energies are those with which divine, cosmic, or God consciousness manifests all creation. Eventually, then, when you connect with others, the basis of that connection comes from the awareness that you and the other are one and the same creation; that any sense of separation is merely an illusion built into the physical constructs of space and time.

"'Some people may try to grasp this intellectually, but all the intellect can do is comprehend it as a concept. True understanding will not occur with any degree of effort on the part of the intellect, but rather through allowing yourself to resonate with those subtle energies. And this results from a spiritual practice that promotes the balanced and harmonic movement of our energies through our bodies to open and fully engage all our force centers. Many of these practices—like yoga, meditation, breath control, energy manipulation, and devotion—are ancient, and have enabled dedicated men and women for thousands of years to develop very high states of consciousness and attain extraordinary powers over matter and energy. The practices have enabled many more to develop an inner peace and harmony, increase their spiritual awareness, connect in a deeper and more satisfying way with others, and set them more firmly on the path that ultimately leads to their own total awareness and liberation.

"'If we allow that the act of expressing gratitude raises one's energy, what do you think is its opposite, and what would diminish one's energy? All our actions and thoughts that are purely self-directed, selfish, and self-interested keep us locked in isolation and separation. They keep us focused on our superficial differences and prevent us from connecting based on our commonalities with all others. Such behavior stems from a zero-sum understanding of energy, joy, and love. That is, people believe that these are commodities which exist in limited supply. As a result, they think they must ration them, because there's only so much to go around. So if they see someone in need of more energy, joy, or love, they must give of their own supply, or, in other words, diminish whatever amount of these they have. Conversely if someone feels he is in need of more energy or love, he must somehow take it from another. Such thinking, however, can never ultimately provide enough of the so-called commodity nor truly satisfy people. Instead they only end up in a relentless pursuit of energy grabbing. This behavior is essentially destructive, because it creates a vibration which becomes strongly reinforced and communicated throughout the world and the universe, that growth and development are only available to a limited number of people, and, regardless of who those few happen to be, everyone else must receive less, ultimately to perish.

"'Observe people interacting with each other, and you can always discern an energy exchange of some type. If you don't mind, I'll borrow from Ardana's example of Mary and John. Mary, in her need to feel stronger, takes energy from John. She succeeds in a very limited sense, in that she momentarily feels better, but at a tremendous cost to John, who has been diminished in the process. Feeling better becomes positive reinforcement for Mary, who proceeds to abuse others for her own enrichment. Her behavior becomes terribly destructive not only for others but even more so for herself. While she may temporarily feel better, she may also lock herself into a behavior that diminishes increasing numbers of others, and, more importantly, reinforces her own limitations. Regardless of how much energy we may take from others, it is minuscule compared with what we receive when we open up to the limitless source of creative energy available to everybody. Mary's behavior not only closes her down to tapping into this unlimited supply, but also creates resentment in those she has diminished. This resentment, because of the vibrational resonance phenomenon Ardana discussed, gets reflected back to Mary, encasing her ever more within a hardened armor of limitation. It can become a vicious and negatively spiraling movement of awareness that leads to extreme isolation, bitterness, and dislike of others.

"'The behavioral pattern that appears opposite to Mary's but is essentially the same is the person who, instead of trying to take energy from others, freely gives her own. Because this one also has not opened up to the infinite source, as she gives to others, she diminishes herself. She is motivated, perhaps, by a misguided sense of noble sacrifice, whereas, in fact, a disguised resentment of those to whom she gives colors her energy, and comes back to her, as in Mary's case, only to isolate and embitter her further.

"'This dynamic, of course, is played in countless ways, by all manner of behavior that stems from zero-sum awareness. In the behavioral pattern that is truly opposite, the individual opens up her energy channel to the infinite source. Then, in her connection with another, as she feeds out energy, she is immediately re-supplied. The result, in some sense, is to feel larger than life, because at that moment, she really is experiencing the source of life itself. Instead of sowing resentment in others, she facilitates their own ability to open up. Moreover when two people's energies are open to and consequently united in that infinite source, then their power substantively increases beyond the mere addition of the two. The potential for true magic exists in this condition, because the individuals have now tapped into consciousness beyond physical limitations. This power increases exponentially with every additional person united in sharing in the infinite source of energy. This was the awareness the twelve of us had from the beginning of our alliance and why we have progressed so far.'

"'So, Jandara,' I asked her, 'when someone like Mary engages us with the intent of enhancing her energy at our expense, how do we act?'

"'This is why our own practice, Narada, is so important. With awareness we understand other people's destructive games and how they attempt to engage us. Then, with sufficient spiritual practice, when someone starts in on us, we open up our own heart chakra and higher energy centers until we are connected to the infinite source. As a result, we don't become diminished by the other person. On the contrary, the other person gets what she needs, and probably more, no resentment is built up, and you create the possibility of increasing her own awareness by moving her energy from a downward to an upward direction.

"'Let's try another exercise like we did earlier. Close your eyes, and center yourself again through the breathing, scanning, and letting go of tension. Recall an event, as before, in which you felt diminished by someone else putting you down through intimidation, yelling, reprimanding, insulting you, or any other of the numerous ways people can do it. Stay with that, and observe how you feel. Now recall an event in which someone extended himself or herself to you, perhaps doing you a favor or an act of kindness that you really appreciated, and in return you felt a deep gratitude. How are you feeling now, and how is your energy moving from what you first felt?'

"Two things became clear from Jandara's guided exercise. First, it was obvious that the two scenarios made me feel totally different; from feeling low, weak, unlovable, worthless, alone, and isolated to experiencing the exact opposite of those feelings. The second was the way I could move my energy depending on the emotional state I focused on.

"'Now,' Jandara continued, 'stay with these good feelings you have, as we focus on something else. This time try and open up to the very source of energy itself. Imagine a tremendous love, the capacity of which is unlimited and completely unconditional. The more you open up to it, the more that pours in. It fills every single cell and every single organ in your body with its inexhaustible supply. It doesn't demand anything of you, as it is completely fulfilled just by being able to express itself through you. Let it flow in, then out, and place no restrictions on where it should go. Don't seek to analyze or understand it; just connect and be with it.'

"I didn't need any more prompting at that point. I had moved into one of the most blissful and expansive states I had ever experienced. I felt a deep and radiating joy that pulsated endlessly in all directions. I felt like a god, with the alchemist's power to turn sorrow into joy. I realized that all limitations were needless constructs composed of disconnected and negative emotions.

"'Wonderful, Narada! Remain with that consciousness. Whenever you become aware of a thought, let it come, let it go, and bring your awareness back to God Consciousness. See that Consciousness as the essence and creator of all that is. Know that there is absolutely nothing in the whole universe that is not of that same essence and creation, and that everything takes its unique form and character as a result of the intelligence in that Consciousness.'

"I heard Jandara's voice and I was aware that for the first time, I didn't become engaged in the thought of the words, the voice that expressed them, or the content of their message. Within and throughout all of this ran the seamless web of a single conscious intelligence, of which I was part, and totally undifferentiated from any other. I no longer was the identity that saw itself with a body and a name and a history, but rather just one of infinite expressions of that single consciousness. Without mass, weight, time, length, width, color, smell, velocity, or even feeling, I was beyond being measured by anyone of these; yet, nonetheless, I gave them all meaning.

"'Narada, you know I can talk to you, and you can remain in total cosmic, or God, consciousness. Eventually, whatever is going on around you, you will be able to remain in that consciousness. That is the goal of your life. That, in fact, is the purpose of every life: That everyone of us fully realize God Consciousness and allow it to express itself at all times with absolutely no qualification from our ego sense of separate identity. You will learn more about this later, but now, I want you to do another exercise.'

"I realized I had become attached to Jandara's words while she was talking and was no longer in that state of undifferentiated consciousness. What remained, however, were the knowledge and the memory of that state. Jandara said that it was from repeated returning to that consciousness that strengthened and reinforced its memory, as well as the ease and quickness to get back in it. She said that there seemed to be no end of the things in life that distract us and mask the true light of our being. And to the extent of our attachment to and identity with these things, whatever joy, happiness, and delight we experience from them, we eventually also experience some degree of discontent, worry, anxiety, and sadness. That is, everything that is not observed with God Consciousness contains its opposite expression. It is precisely this sense of duality that characterizes the normal consciousness of human kind, and from which we will all eventually attain God Consciousness. She emphasized how important it was for people to let go of all associations they may have with the words *God, cosmic,* or whatever the particular word and its associations might be, as the energy this mental activity created effectively blocked the individual from entering into the expansive state that led to unity consciousness.

"'Narada, what I'd like you to do now is remember a deep love relationship you've had in your life; how it began and how it ended. Return to it and capture its predominant feelings again with your whole being.'

"Whether fortunate or not probably depends more on the particular individual, but I could, in fact, recall two such affairs that very deeply engaged my heart. While the two sat at opposite ends of the spectrum in terms of length of the relationship and level of commitment, both moved my heart with emotions so strong that left me their slave. Both opened up in me a passion so consuming that the only visage I could entertain was my lover's. And both, when they became one sided—or when I finally opened my eyes and allowed myself to realize that they had become or perhaps always were one sided (the fire of my passion consuming dry ice)—my passion turned to pain. A pain so deep it mocks you with its capacity; you fear you may suffocate in its depths.

"I captured those feelings all right and once again felt the icy grip of rejection clutch around my heart and snuff out every last burning ember. A ruined structure whose appeal could only delight a romantic archeologist, my heart had little left to sustain me. I ached again as I had in the past, and felt like a cosmic black hole from which not even a glimmer of hope might emerge.

"'Narada, now allow that pure, unconditional, and infinite source of God Consciousness to pour into your being as before. See how you can choose either to hold on to your suffering or to dissipate its darkness with the unfathomable cosmic light.'

"I did as Jandara instructed and experienced an extraordinary transformation. I went from the depths of despair to the heights of ecstasy. As though a black cloth that had been covering my cage had been lifted, I experienced a new light. In that light the cage became visible for the first time, and I realized that the bars on the cage had not blocked me from leaving, but rather, only served to support the black cloth. I understood from Jandara's teachings that my darkness and despair were a natural consequence of believing myself an identity separate from God Consciousness; that in some perverse way I had held up my suffering as a trophy to show others the depth of my passion and what a noble victim I had been. A mild but largely useless tonic is how Jandara described it and one that does nothing to move us along the spiritual path. She said it's important to realize that every time you find there's something you don't like, makes you angry, fearful, insecure, worried, or anxious, you're in duality thinking. Learn to make the association with God Consciousness at that point, and allow it to flood your being.

"'Well, Narada, you certainly have been on an emotional roller-coaster today, but at least now you understand how energy can move through your body, and you can either passively allow it to happen, or actively direct its course. You also saw the difference between duality thinking that comes from separation consciousness, and unity thinking that comes from being in God Consciousness. Attaining total cosmic consciousness is not the privilege of a few enlightened beings, but rather the innate potential inherent in every person, awaiting patiently throughout the ages to be realized by them. Only by awakening to that potential, then practicing allowing it to express itself, can we finally throw off the shroud of darkness surrounding our cages and experience the liberation and freedom that is our birthright.'

"We ended for the day at this point because it was already very late in the afternoon, and the others would soon be arriving. I felt the exhilaration that often accompanies fatigue after a rigorous workout and looked forward to the relaxing fun that we all always enjoyed together in the evenings."

Chapter Five

A Trip to the Lowlands

"The next morning I woke up much earlier than usual for some reason. When I went to the temple I wondered if Jandara would be with me again. Instead, Arzano, who had previously helped me in my arrangements to stay, and Manora now greeted me. 'So, are you ready to leave, Narada?' I had absolutely no idea what she was talking about, and the quizzical expression on my face communicated as much. 'Didn't Jandara tell you?' Arzano added. 'We thought you might like a change of scenery and decided to go into town.'

"The idea of going into town on a pleasure trip was a thought I had never even entertained. Being back on the mountain top I had become, I guess, disconnected with the everyday life of typical people and events. I had no idea where the closest town was nor how one could even get there. Manora dispersed my puzzlement and described the arrangements. 'There's a winding foot path that leads midway down to a clearing where, once a week, a bus takes a meandering route throughout the region to bring farmers into the town. If we leave in five minutes we can make it without rushing.' I hadn't finished eating, but Arzano suggested I take my food and eat it along the way.

"Although the idea was sudden, I immediately looked forward to some new sights and a 'day off,' or so I thought. A short walk across our site soon turned into a steep, rugged, and winding descent. I feared the difficulty I encountered would pale compared to the return ascent, and felt somewhat alone in my awkward maneuvers, as Arzano and Manora nimbly ambled down. They kept up a running conversation which I had trouble tuning into as I remained focused on not twisting an ankle. My growing fatigue seemed to slow down time, and I increasingly wondered if we were really walking all the way into town. I tried to maintain my interest and momentum by picking up curiously shaped and colored rocks I found along the path. Eventually, however, we arrived at a small clearing beside a hard-packed dirt road, and my hopes that this would be our waiting spot were justified. There was no marker, nor was anyone else around waiting, but I gratefully accepted that our peregrination had ended. Our wait for the bus was short lived. I had no sooner plopped myself on the ground and emitted a groan of relief when it pulled up.

"The bus was old and rickety. It had a pale yellow color, and I wondered if it were a discarded school bus hand-me-down from the U.S. The once brightly colored decorations suspended around the driver evidenced the ravages of time, and the dust that the wheels kicked up covered both inside and outside with little consideration. About half the seats were already taken. We moved down the obstacle-course of an aisle past assorted objects–including enormous stuffed cloth bags, a worn tire, and a live turkey–toward the back of the bus where we could all sit together. The other passengers were quiet and showed little interest in us. Except for a few children, the ages both of the men and women seemed indeterminate. Their worn faces had a dark complexion, and their creases reminded me of a dry river delta.

"While I was glad I finally got to sit, even that soon proved tiresome. My vertical motion as each bump and hole bounced me in the air was only exceeded by the horizontal sway. The seats having long lost any cushioning they once may have had, the springs having degenerated into blunt knife points, I quickly abandoned any notion that I was out on a pleasure trip. I desperately scrutinized the faces of my friends in search of a sign that my discomfort had some company, but my agony found no companions. Instead it selfishly commanded all my attention and left no room for any thoughts of a loftier nature. My only gratitude came from not having a problem with hemorrhoids. What little comfort that thought embraced me, however, was soon overcome with an anger-colored annoyance. About the time that color got particularly strong, Arzano leaned over to me and seemingly out of the blue quietly said in a sing-song voice 'Careful what you wish for....' I had no idea what he was talking about, and my anger blocked any mental processing. I was more inclined to communicate with the empty seat next to me with a pounding blow from my fist but didn't want to demonstrate so overtly how I was losing it.

"Further along the road we came to another stop. I would soon realize how short sighted it had been to think things couldn't get any worse. What attracted my attention before I even saw the man waiting to get on was the cloud of dust he kicked up all around him. I had no sooner begun to wonder about it when I noticed upon our approach the circles he circumscribed in the air with his rope that beat into the ground with every swing. Great, I thought, just what we need—some cattle-less lasso-loco to stir up the bus! He hopped on with long macho strides. With a swagger that brought him slowly up the aisle, he was either performing for the other passengers, or checking each one out; probably the former, as his drunken demeanor appeared to leave him bereft of any mental functioning. He seemed to capture no one's interest, as the others either found the view outside more arresting or were lost in their own space. My companions were amused as they might be at the circus. I, alone, seemed to find in him another source of annoyance and another element to add to my discomfort. With every step he took toward the back I heard myself silently shouting that he sit down; every inch closer ratcheted up my anxiety. I wished I had brought a bag to occupy the empty seat next to me and in its absence tried to spread my own body across it.

"My efforts were in vain. Without looking at or acknowledging my presence in any way he pushed past and unloaded his foul smelling carcass right next to me. Turning my back to him as best I could did little to stifle his obnoxious behavior. Either moved by his own boredom or the perverse delight his irritating behavior brought him, Lasso-loco soon began his rope play again. Each swing brushed against my leg and scattered dust. Each swing was followed with a crooning moan and broadcast his foul breath. I thought we couldn't reach our destination fast enough. You can imagine my own delight, therefore, when a clearing we turned into announced the first outlines of a town.

"I expected our approach would find him scrambling out of his seat to be the first one off. A curious thing occurred, however, which seemed to make suffering him almost worth it. How he managed to do it, I couldn't possibly figure out, and was too delighted to care. As we pulled up to our final stop and people began to gather up their belongings, Lasso-loco had succeeded in ensnaring himself in his own rope. It had become wrapped around his torso, through the metal hand rail in front of him, around his leg, and caught somehow in the springs below the seat. His yelling only evoked laughter from the others as they left, and as we filed past, his fury entangled him further. Only as we distanced ourselves from the bus did his cries seem to diminish, and I wondered how long he managed to keep them up.

"My mood changed dramatically with this incident. I was extremely happy to be off that ride from hell and away from the devil's trouble-maker. As we walked toward the plaza Arzano once again directed his sing-song voice toward me saying, 'Cause you just may get it.' I was completely taken aback by his statement, but knew he was too advanced a master to display a loose screw. 'Do you think it was just bad luck that your friend sat next to you,' Arzano continued. I started to protest that the lunatic wasn't my friend when Arzano cut me off. 'Like anyone else in the world, that guy was looking for companionship. Like most people he unconsciously sought out an energy configuration that harmonized with his own. No one else on the bus, as you also noticed, could be bothered by him. They remained unperturbed, calm, and centered. You, however, wanted some diversion from your extreme discomfort and unsettled mind. You got your diversion all right, and like a magnet, your agitated energy drew him directly to you. I tried to warn you before he got on the bus. I hoped a gentle reminder would have been sufficient to get you to redirect your energy and settle down.'

"I felt a bit chagrined and tried to make light of it by remarking how it was almost worth it to have seen that guy get caught up in his own trap. 'You have Manora to thank for that.' I glanced over to Manora with a questioning look to which she responded only with a smile and a twinkle in her eye. Arzano replied for her. 'She guided his rope with her energy and conscious thought in order both to teach him a lesson and to rescue you. Otherwise he'd still be here hanging around and annoying you, and, who knows...you may even have come to blows with him.' Then Manora added cryptically, 'And maybe there was a lesson in there for you too.'

"I fell silent as we continued to walk and thought about the events of the morning and how my energy changed. I recalled what Arzano had said about my energy having attracted that guy to me, and then remembered that incident from my past when I had left my apartment in an agitated and angry state and, according to Jandara, brought that knife attack upon us.

"'Do you see,' Arzano continued, 'how external events can jerk us around like puppets on strings? Had you reminded yourself early this morning about the true nature of your being, you could have immediately prevented the downward spiraling of negative energy. We know this is very difficult, as we had worked on it consciously a very long time. Nevertheless only this awareness will enable people to reverse the direction of control of those puppet strings. People have become so attached to everything in their human condition that their identity becomes glued to it. Whether what happens to them is good or bad they immediately identify with it and insist on possessing it. They want to own everything. People can not truly own anything once they realize that everything is just a manifestation of Supreme Consciousness. When you mistake the image in the mirror for the real thing, then you're just chasing a mirage. When you insist on owning your reflection in the water you will drown.'

"'Why should this awareness be so illusive and difficult to attain?' I asked Arzano. 'Habit,' he said. 'Habit and teaching. We are not like this when we are born. Because our physical senses are not fully developed when we newly incarnate, our knowledge of the world around us is more direct than that of the adults around us. Our psychic sense at that stage is dominant, which enables us to have an acute sense of the emotions of those around us. Although we take on a new brain when we incarnate our soul retains its psychic mode of communication and interaction. This is why newborns and young children perceive and respond to entities that adults claim are non-existent.

"As children grow, their physical senses develop. The adults around the children reward them for their response to and recognition of objects and events in the physical world and simultaneously discourage and disparage children's psychic interaction and play. Our physical senses respond to physical boundaries, and as the senses develop children learn that boundaries are associated with ownership, individuality, and identity. Through constant patterning of positive and negative reinforcements children grow into adults who can only see and respond to the material world and believe that it is the essence of reality. From this as their basic frame of reference they construct theories and models that try to explain physical and human behavior. To others seeing from the same frame of reference such explanations make perfect sense and become dogma.

Unfortunately their dogma also becomes their shackles and keeps them tied to their boundaries, separation, and isolation. In this bounded condition they become their own puppets. And, I haven't even begun to mention the effects of karma.'

"'Well,' I countered, 'the picture you paint certainly makes it seem hopeless that anybody could possibly change and develop a different awareness!'

"'That's not entirely correct, but it certainly appears that human evolution is a very long and drawn-out process. Some people do become aware and wake up to their essential nature. And this has been happening for thousands of years. When that occurs and they attain more advanced states, they become teachers to help others along. Of course there are those who reverse the process. That is, they play the role of teacher to convince others of their supposed attainments. Such behavior, however, stems from ego delusions of separation consciousness. Bogus teachers feign superiority from selfish, ulterior motives of personal gain and self-enhancement. True teachers open up their hearts to divine love and let Supreme Consciousness guide their thoughts and actions. They have nothing to gain from their actions because from the state of Divine Consciousness from which they operate nothing is lost and nothing is gained.

"'But it is true that people are slow to learn. Their habits create deep grooves in their emotional and mental bodies that channel energy in certain, prescribed ways, much as a canyon constrains the flow of water. Getting the energy to flow in new and different directions means creating new channels. This means creating new habits to forge new energy channels. This is what is so difficult. It takes energy, time, and commitment to create new channels. When people are fatigued and constrained by the difficulties and obstacles of daily living, they have little or no energy left for creating anything new in their lives. Moreover, and perhaps most importantly, the process takes belief.

"'There has to be some reason for people to change. They have to believe there is another way of being. Sometimes people have the example of an individual who has shown some amazing quality or ability which serves them inspirationally as a direction to grow. Others get glimpses of their own divine nature which filters through the holes and gaps created from the discontent with the ordinariness, emptiness, or general dissatisfaction with their lives. Some may then turn to substances like drugs and alcohol to amplify those glimpses. While potentially effective in the short run, the continued use of such substances generally prevents new and natural energy channels from forming. Despite the obvious side effects, these substances may force energy into psychic areas in which people are not prepared to handle, or open up areas that require spiritual strength and stamina to withstand. As in allowing a child into a chemistry laboratory, huge forces can be unwittingly unleashed with grave consequences.

"'In addition to the belief that their lives can be different, people have to believe that only a sustained practice will get them there. New canyons must be carved. People must create new channels for the energy to flow a different way. When the energy is not forced but allowed and encouraged to flow along a different route, then the body can withstand the changes of awareness and power that come as a result of the energy opening up previously dormant centers of the energetic body.

"'The practices that enable these changes are things like meditation, various controlled breathing techniques, reading, and contemplating the written works of sages that can reflect their own, innate nature, and keeping the company of other illuminated and wise people.

"'Patience in allowing themselves to develop spiritually to the point that changes become obvious is one of the major obstacles people face in their practice. This is especially true in many of today's societies, like your own, where everything runs at such a fast pace and everyone expects instant results. It is not uncommon for people to begin a practice with the sincere intention of developing their spiritual awareness only to quit shortly afterwards because no obvious gain became apparent. When people proceed with this purpose they demonstrate the material consciousness their practice is intended to transcend.'

"Throughout Arzano's discourse the three of us meandered around the streets of the town devoid of destination. I particularly enjoyed the steady walk on even ground after the morning's mountain descent and the bus ride. Eventually Manora motioned us over to the town plaza where we could sit and watch the local goings-on. We sat in silence for a while just to observe the place and the people. The plaza was typical for those small towns. It took up a whole block and was surrounded by small stores across each street. A statue of a military general atop a pedestal adorned the center of the plaza from which walkways extended spoke-like toward the perimeter. The small shrubs that lined the walkways formed a visual protection around the myriad flowers planted inside. A scattering of wooden benches could be found set in from the walkways with the same shrubs surrounding the two sides and back of the benches. Other benches formed a large circle around the general. Many tall and broad-limbed trees provided both shade from the intense sun and sanctuary for the numerous birds whose melodiousness complemented the serene ambiance.

"While certainly not crowded, a number of people, mostly older men and women and some young children, could be found at various benches. We sat at a bench inside the circle. Although I was inclined just to kick back and relax, Arzano directed me to actively observe the energy flow between the people as they interacted with each other. I felt uncertain as I didn't quite know what to look at and wasn't able to actually see the energy as they could. Arzano said that as the physical body manifested the flow of energy I should train my eyes to observe all shifts in bodily movement from the most blunt to the most fine, including the myriad subtle changes in facial expression. 'It's impossible for people to hide the expression of their energy,' he said. 'People often think they can, only because most other people are not very adept at reading it, at least not at the very subtle levels. Your lie-detector machine works because it's able to record some of the fine, physiological changes that occur as a result of energy shifts. In order for you to observe these changes yourself you must become a very sensitive receptor. Like a speaker diaphragm that vibrates as a result of the very specific signals it receives, you must train your own emotional diaphragm to vibrate to the specific energetic signals it picks up from other people. And, of course, you can't do this when you're absorbed and caught up in your own emotional charges. The interference this produces distorts or blocks what you could pick up from others, in the same way it's difficult to pick up clearly the details of a conversation in a roomful of chatter.'

"I was contemplating what Arzano said and trying to apply it to those in the plaza when suddenly he announced that he and Manora were going to a store across the square to chat with an old acquaintance they noticed had just gone in. Arzano instructed me to wait and practice observing. I was comfortable being by myself and expected nothing unwelcome to occur while they were around.

"On the opposite side of the circle from several children who had been playing quietly together emerged some raucous sounds. I looked over and noticed that one of the boys began to play the role of bully, shoving and lording over the others. Perhaps not an uncommon scene and one found the world over, yet it affected me in an unexpected manner. I recalled a similar time in my own life when I became the object of the neighborhood bully. I had never thought of that occasion until that moment in the plaza. It brought back more than just the thought. I experienced a tightness in my chest and throat and a shaking throughout my body. I don't know how long I was caught up in that mental and physical memory but was quickly jarred out of it by a swift kick I received in the side of my leg. As I looked up some foul-smelling miscreant barked out a crude greeting. He sat next to me and continued uttering a mixture of obscenities and crazy, disconnected statements, although I understood little of his mumbling. I wanted just to get away from him, when it occurred to me that this guy must be either Arzano or Manora in one of their great disguises I had learned they were capable of enacting. It became perhaps too obvious that the reason they walked away was to cook up this scenario to teach me a lesson.

"With this awareness of what they were doing my energy shifted and I became confident. I put out my arm to shove him over and said: 'Nice outfit, but did you have to stink yourself up so bad!' He slapped my arm away in such a forceful manner I let out a yell. I looked around to see if anyone had been watching our little drama, but saw that no one was looking over at all. I got annoyed and told him to cool the act. His response, which I finally understood and realized he had been saying all along, was to demand my money. I was looking away from him acting unconcerned when a flash of light caught the corner of my eye. In the same movement that brought my head around to realize the origin of that flash was the sunlight reflecting off the knife he had pulled out, I also saw Arzano and Manora emerge from the store they had entered and turn the corner into the side street.

"The impulse to yell out through my wall of terror was instantly subverted by a sharp sting I felt on my side. I looked down and saw blood oozing where he had sliced through my pants, probably hoping to get what he thought was money or valuables stuffed in my pocket. I quickly gave a startled gasp as I looked past his shoulder in order to distract him long enough so I could pull out the contents of my pocket that he had opened up. I took the little bundle of stones I had earlier collected and wrapped in a rag to keep them from rattling around and hurled it right at his face when he turned back. With the moment this bought me I took off like a bat out of hell.

"He came tearing after me. I had no idea where I was headed but I was fueled by my fear and guided by my need just to get away from him. I ran down a deserted street and hoped that when I dodged into another I would have lost him. My fleeting wish quickly turned impotent when I glanced back and saw him still on my heels. At the next corner the street merged into a field that lay at the edge of town and I continued my course across it. All of a sudden I found the terror had left me and I was gliding along in a state of relaxed amusement. Then it hit me that I had left my body, and like those few times from my past, found myself sailing through the air above myself. I looked down and observed this thrilling scene of someone chasing after my body, which seemed to know exactly how and where to move.

"I followed as the two raced across the field and into another street back toward the plaza. Shortly after my body turned another corner I was quickly brought back into it as I stumbled over some people walking across the street. I lost my balance and came crashing to the ground. I looked up and through my stunned gaze thought I saw Manora and Arzano walking toward me. The rascal had disappeared and probably took off when he saw I was not alone. 'Out jogging?' Arzano joked. 'I thought you had just wanted to sit and relax!' I wasn't amused and kept quiet.

"Manora knelt down when she noticed my blood-stained pants. The gash was deeper than I had realized. Blood was still oozing out, and the area around the wound was chaffed from the run and the rubbing against the clothes. I figured I needed to get it cleaned and bandaged as soon as possible. When I tried to get up, however, she held me down with one arm and a force I found completely unexpected. She placed her other hand right over my wound and held it there. An intense radiation poured out of her hand and spread throughout my whole body. All my agitation seemed to drain away along with my fatigue, and I began to feel charged and euphoric.

"After a while Manora removed her hand and stood up. I could feel the blood had stopped, but when I looked down to examine my wound I saw that my pants were no longer torn. The only evidence of damage was a tiny seam where the tear had been and a blood stain. Well, I don't know if it was the wildly astonished expression on my face or my action that followed it but they both burst into uncontrollable laughter. Since I couldn't observe my wound now through my mended pants, I quickly pulled them down to examine it. All that remained was the stain of blood. I rubbed some of it off with saliva in search of some other evidence that I had been gashed but could find nothing. Pointing to the stain on my pants, Manora said, 'Sorry, I don't do stains,' which occasioned another outburst from the two of them.

"For some strange reason they both seemed rather unconcerned with what I had just gone through, even though I felt I might have been either killed or badly hurt. I couldn't help but think they may have been somehow connected to it, even though I knew neither of them was the maniac rogue in disguise. Yet I didn't dwell on this thought because I was so awed by Manora's healing power. I had never experienced anything so dramatic. This would be, however, only the first of other extraordinary examples of healing I would witness.

"Arzano helped me off the ground and announced it was time to head back, since the bus only made one return trip a day. The dread of discomfort that I had feared would accompany me on the return trip never materialized. I remained charged with energy the whole time and experienced a heightened sense of blissful awareness. Either I was still feeling the forceful effects of Manora's work on me or the two of them conspired to help me along. On the bus ride they maneuvered to be on either side of me, and on the ascent up the mountain one remained in front and the other behind me. Despite my good feelings, the welcome sight of our home awakened me to my extreme fatigue. Arzano threw out in his uniquely wily way that my next trip should be easier. I looked at him in anticipation of further explanation, but as it was not forthcoming, and since I was too tired to press, I easily let it go. My bed was extremely attractive that night, and I relished the rest it would bring me.

Chapter Six

A Visit to Carana

"I woke up the next morning refreshed as a newborn. I was looking forward to whatever teachings a new day would bring and wondered who my teacher might be. With my morning routine at last completed, I made my way down toward the temple. The moment I entered the temple, the sight of Rolana allowed the imprint of a vivid dream I had had that night to come and flood my waking consciousness. I stood as if frozen as the images came rushing back.

"In the dream Adonara and I were on a bus coming down from the mountain headed into town. The bus was about half full, and from our location in the back we had a clear view of the rest of the passengers. We were amusing ourselves with a little game by examining and comparing the colors and shapes of the energy surrounding the other people. Our little entertainment more than helped move the time along, as it also served to develop our facility for seeing auras and energy.

"Generally there were no colors of particular brilliance or shapes with any clear definition surrounding the passengers. Spaced out the window they all seemed just to want to relax without the burden of some clear mental focus. All but two, that is. Besides the driver, who seemed focused on the road, one passenger who sat alone yet in the middle of all the others began to emanate a very strong energy field. It was actually disturbing to look at. The color was predominantly a coarse and grayish green with streaks of brown swirling around within a nebulous shaped cloud, and from which piercing hooked arrows darted out toward the rest of the passengers. His intent, we thought, was to direct a mental image to the others for some devious end; an easy situation for someone with sufficient mental control and a group as receptive as these.

"Shortly the bus stopped and, as if on cue, all the passengers got up and left the bus. Although we had anticipated something might occur, the subsequent events followed swiftly and unexpectedly. In that space of time in which surprise yields to realization, the fiend and his accomplice—the bus driver—had completely overtaken and tied us up. Their last act before exiting the bus was to release the breaks and let it roll down the mountain. Without allowing ourselves to succumb to the horror of the situation we merged our mental focus and with the combined force of our emotional power guided the bus through the steep and meandering road.

"The road finally gave up its incline to the flatness of the valley plain. Having earlier run out of gas only gravity fueled the bus down the mountain until it coasted to a dead stop. An approaching car that moved into view the moment we entered the plain reached us the moment we stopped. As though guided to our rescue, the man and the woman from that car released us from our shackles, emptied the contents of their gas can into the bus, and immediately drove away—all of this performed in complete silence. We then drove the bus into town, and with the danger now behind us, tried to understand what had just occurred. We became baffled when a familiarity regarding this couple dawned on our consciousness and evoked a charge of alarm, despite their having come to our aid. Our consternation augmented further with the feeling that these two were somehow connected with the driver and his accomplice. We drove the bus directly into the center of town and parked at the edge of the main square. When we got off we saw, sitting on a bench directly in front of us as though awaiting our arrival, Rolana.

"'Good morning, Narada. You look at me as though I were a ghost! It's really me, I'm really here, and this is not a dream.'

"Despite the warm welcome Rolana extended to me, I didn't respond, paralyzed into silence as though caught between two worlds. Or rather two realities that suddenly seemed less distinct than ever before. Was I experiencing an expanding consciousness that encompassed new information; an enlarged field of awareness unconcerned with the boundaries circumscribing former knowledge fields? If what you know is the numerator and what you don't know is the denominator, then when you increase your field of knowledge, have you increased the numerator or the denominator? Yet while thoughts such as these turned their mental somersaults I felt a pulsing field of energy around me, as though those very movements were the breathing of a higher consciousness. The sense that I had formerly had of myself, my sense of 'I,' receded, becoming an evanescent blossom of my total being; the enchanting perfume that lives from one flower to another and lingers after the last yet remains encoded until nurtured back into sweetness at a later time. Like the multitude of pollen that scatters in all directions, my thoughts were no less an integral part of the flower yet remained an infinitesimally small part of total being.

"In the shifting of my awareness—an event that was becoming increasingly common for me—I noticed I was sitting across from Rolana at the table now spread with our breakfast. A shimmering light surrounded her body and framed a face of complete serenity. The hunger that informed me that this flower needed nourishing did so gently, seemingly content in expressing its purpose. I honored it as I ate, feeling that my own joy was similarly expressing a small part of something much greater.

"'Narada, your accomplishment in attaining and maintaining Divine consciousness is evident; faster than our already high expectations of you. Although you've been with us only a short time, it's been like an intensive workshop. You've benefited from the single-minded focus on your spiritual development without any of the distractions that normally rant and rave in people's heads and demand attention. Moreover, being in our company, surrounded by our energies and the energy of our home base has enabled you to raise the vibrational level of your own energy.

"'You know from your basic studies in physics how objects and people tend to resonate together. For example, a group of pendulums set in motion at different intervals will eventually swing in unison as if they were all attached. Likewise you may have heard how a group of women living together can eventually synchronize their monthly cycles. These, and infinitely more examples, are very normal phenomena and demonstrate the natural attraction between all objects and people. This affinity occurs because in reality, everything that exists has the same origin. This origin is the glue that holds everything together. While you may be able to find examples of forces that exist in opposition to one another, that opposition is also just another manifestation of the One Source.

"'This affinity doesn't mean, of course, that the state of peace and harmony is necessarily common and widespread. On the contrary it generally appears that the opposite is true. Where is the individual who has not participated in or witnessed the seemingly endless antagonism, strife, and warfare that tears apart couples, families, communities, states, and nations? To most people, the notion of natural attraction must seem idealistic or naive. The chaos that characterizes so many people's lives, however, hardly registers as cosmic noise, in relation to the vast, endless, and mighty universe. From the state of ego-centered consciousness the smallest human events assume huge proportions, whereas from the consciousness of the infinite cosmos, even the most major events of people's lives cause barely a ripple.

"'Nevertheless, this is not to say that anything goes; to sanction all behavior. All the events of our lives, including all our actions, thoughts and feelings, are important and consequential. They have very real results, whose outcomes affect our ability to transcend our limitations and attain the liberation and freedoms associated with divine, cosmic, and unity consciousness. When I speak about affinity, therefore, I mean the effect of sympathetic resonance that enables the vibrations of one entity to attract another entity of similar quality, or cause another entity to move into its own vibrational state. This is how people affect each other. To the degree of strength we exhibit a particular emotion, we can either move others into our own emotional state or be moved into theirs. This is why the company we keep is so important. Your being with us now has enabled you to move quickly into higher spiritual attainment as a result of the resonance of our much higher vibrational energy. The darker and more negative energy of discord and disharmony that often surrounded you, and generally surrounds most people, retards spiritual growth. To leap out of such a soup of chaos and confusion requires tremendous energy, and to stay out of it requires the sustained support of a higher conscious community. In other words, people need to be impacted regularly with those higher vibrations until they become the dominant mode of resonance in their lives, and hence, self-sustaining.'

"'How do people find and surround themselves with a community of those more spiritually aware?' I asked Rolana.

"'This naturally begins to happen to people when they consciously engage themselves on the path of developing their spiritual understanding. Doing such practices as meditation and yoga, and studying and contemplating sacred writings, enables seekers of the Light to create the vibrational field that attracts not only other seekers, but also circumstances propitious to their development. For example, many seekers know the experiences of chance encounters with someone who can particularly move them forward. Or they strangely stumble across a book that contains exactly what they were looking for to move them up the next rung of their ladder. This phenomenon is not limited just to the area of spiritual development. In fact in any area of our lives, where we focus our attention tends to attract a response from the universe which can respond to the creator of that focus in the most unexpected and mysterious ways. In actuality such occurrences are a natural working out of the vibrational flow of energy created by our ability to focus. Like the laser, which derives its power from being highly focused, our own mental focus will only be as strong and effective as our ability to maintain a sustained and concentrated focus.'

"Rolana's discussion of focus made me realize that I was no longer able to concentrate very well on what she had been saying. Then when I wondered what I might have missed I realized my mind was wandering too much to maintain any focus. She read my energy and stopped to give me a break. When I brought my awareness back to our surroundings, I noticed we were still at the table, although the morning had already given birth to afternoon. Rolana suggested we go for a walk to stretch our legs and get some exercise.

"We started out on a path that I had already explored several times, which provided a measure of comfort that enabled me to engage in a kind of walking meditation. We walked in silence a long time. After some period of time my mind seemed to get more and more empty of thoughts. I became an observer both of my thoughts as well as the process of their arising in my mind and entering my head, then letting them go. I became so clear as to how in my typical consciousness there was no separation between myself and my thoughts. My identification with them was strong and intact and seemed to flow from one thought to another, without stop or pause, and endlessly. Now, in realizing this, I became aware of gaps or spaces between my thoughts: As if I had lived in a dark and narrow barrel all my life going from stave to stave, until one day the wood slowly began to shrink, leaving gaps and scattered spaces; in which light entered and penetrated the darkness like sharp needles; at first revealing very little of what might be inside the barrel, but for the needle that pierced my awareness and made me wonder if such a contrast to darkness existed, what might it possibly be, and how far must it extend? And if I feared this might already be too much to contemplate, then my fear soon turned to awe, as the wood continued to shrink, those spaces between staves increased, and I realized that the potential for possibilities was infinite.

"*How would you like to take a trip, Narada?*'

"I heard her words as the most natural thing in my life, except that Rolana was not using her voice to communicate with me. I looked at her and thought, '*Where to?*'

'*How would you like to visit Carana?*' she thought back to me. The pulsations of joy I emitted were the only answer she needed.

"Immediately I noticed that the outlines of Rolana's body began to fade. It started first with her feet and hands and slowly worked its way up her legs and arms. I was not shocked or surprised, but rather, fascinated. So fascinated, in fact, that I didn't notice for some time that the same thing was happening to me. Then I became absolutely delighted. The most wonderful thing about this whole process is that I never felt separated from Rolana, but felt her next to me the whole time, and we continued to communicate just as we were when seated in the temple.

"After some timeless period neither of us had any physical, bodily form. This didn't disturb me at all. My consciousness seemed perfectly comfortable without the body, as though it just wasn't dependent on it for its survival or sense of self.

"'*Let's see if he has any clients with him before we drop in. I'd hate to unnerve anybody like that, especially when they go to him for healing. What do you see, Narada?*'

"I didn't see anything and didn't quite know where to look. To my thought, she responded, '*It's not a question of where you look, as you do with your physical eyes. It's a question of intent. Intend your attention where you want it, and focus your consciousness there. This should be fairly easy for you because you've been there before.*' As soon as she said this I remembered what I had thought was a day dream that occurred while I was resting on a break during my time with Carana. I did what Rolana suggested and immediately had a vision of Carana in his inner office, and the attendant was in an outer room.

"Immediately we went to his office. Although we didn't materialize, Carana came over and gave us a warm embrace. He did this, however, while leaving his body still in the chair.

"Carana, who loves to amuse himself, transmitted to me: *'Narada, you're becoming quite a regular here,'* to which they both cracked up laughing. I couldn't help being amused either. *'Your timing is excellent! I'm shortly to receive a visit, not from a client, but from an important member of the clergy, here on a mission from the city, checking out reports of heresy and evil craft. The Church in these parts feels a strong need to control these things. Their emissary thinks he's on an important mission for the Church. He doesn't realize there's a much more important reason that only involves him. He's really coming to be healed, but isn't aware of it yet. Obviously you're also here to be part of this, so why don't you appear materially for him as well. He's still a bit short-sighted.'*

"Carana went back to his body, and Rolana materialized both herself and myself. We had no sooner returned to this form when our visitor arrived. He introduced himself as Father Francesco Buonapedire. He was a huge man in height and weight and imposing in demeanor. Backed by the authority of the Church, he played the role of a man of importance, although his feigned nobility poorly masked his condescension. Carana graciously introduced Rolana and me; however, Father Francesco simply dismissed us with a nod that questioned why we were even there. It was obvious from his disposition that he arrived with an agenda from which he intended not to deviate even a fraction. His mission was to get Carana—or rather *Don Miguel*, a humble friar and great healer, as he was known to everybody for miles and miles around—to cease his activities or be excommunicated and banished forever from the area.

"*'Do you recognize this guy, Narada?'* Rolana asked me telepathically. *'There's something familiar about him,* I responded, *but I don't know why.' 'We often saw him during our visits to the village at the time the Spanish were first coming to our shores,'* she told me. *'He was a minor official in the Church, but had great ambitions for his future. His ambitions were so great, in fact, that he double-crossed many of his friends and colleagues, often resulting in dire consequences for them. He paid dearly for this in two subsequent lifetimes, and struggled even more so in the psychic world between those two lives. He came into this lifetime with great promise, although poor guidance along the way reawakened his unresolved ambition. While he is a man of tremendous power, he has often directed it unwisely.*

"'He has now arrived at a point in his life where a deep, inner conflict has manifested. His ambitious side has become increasingly threatened by the development of his own genuine spiritual awareness and a deep desire to help and heal others. He really comes today from an unconscious desire to heal his own conflict, as well as the disharmony he has participated in for so long. The challenge for Carana now is to get Father Francesco to generate the energy necessary to transcend the limitations imposed by his ego desires, so that he becomes completely awake and aware of the consequences of all his actions.'

"While Rolana was giving me this background on Buonapedire, he started on this long tirade against Don Miguel, who remained completely unmoved, but presented a smiling countenance that only infuriated his assailant even more. Buonapedire demanded that Don Miguel immediately cease all healing activities or he would personally persecute the 'supposed' healer to such a degree he would come to him on his knees begging for the persecution to stop. Father Francesco became so excited, in fact, that all of a sudden he collapsed on the floor writhing in pain. He reached out his hand gesturing for help, but Don Miguel remained as unmoved as before. Father Francesco's agony was so great at that point that he just passed out. Then Carana said, 'Now the real fun begins!'

"I didn't know what he meant by that, but it didn't take long to find out. Immediately the four of us were transported to a totally different scene. We remained as outside observers watching as a newly initiated young Father Francesco sat helpless on the bed of his ailing mother as she pleaded with him to heal her. 'Help me, Cesco,' she wailed. 'Aren't you now a priest? Why can't you help me.' She moaned on and on like this for hours, until she finally passed away. Her face, so contorted from her agony that she no longer looked the same, only expressed contempt for her son's helplessness.

"Instantly the scene shifted. This time the four of us witnessed a young man being flogged by a functionary of the local church, under the orders of Father Francesco Buonapedire early in his career, who stood by rubbing his hands together, almost in ecstatic enjoyment and expectancy of his rising fame. The young man had been accused of a minor offense, one that certainly did not merit such punishment, but Buonapedire saw an opportunity to advance his own standing within the hierarchy. The Father with us now looked on in obvious discomfort.

"Buonapedire started to say something to us but before he could the scene shifted for a third time. We found ourselves this time inside the home of one of the few very wealthy families of the region. Darkness and despair dominated every corner of the mansion. The shades were drawn in every room. Family members slumped languidly on the chairs and sofas in the parlor too worried to talk but too anxious to be silent; the result of which were half sentences, disconnected phrases, and hollow cries that seemed to drop from the mournful air like sap dripping from a dying tree. The cause of all this distress was the landowner's wife, who lay comatose on her bed, the result of a fall she suffered on her way to church when the horse, startled by some unseen specter, reared up and overturned the carriage she was riding in.

"She was a very caring person, loved by all who came in contact with her, and even by many who never met her, but who benefited from her charity. She was a very religious person, but had grown increasingly disenchanted with the Church, its rigidity, and the hypocrisy she encountered. Her husband, a wealthy landowner, was an important supporter of the Church, although his main interest in it was political. Spiritually he was as connected as the cathedral's flying buttress whose only function was decorative. Nevertheless, he loved his wife dearly and felt he couldn't carry on without her.

"Now he paced the room from one end to the other and back again. He had brought in the most important doctors from the whole region. Each went through the same ritual of examining her, asking questions, employing known techniques, and suggesting various remedies, but nothing proved effective and her condition worsened. As each doctor came and went, an inner conflict visibly tore him up inside. He knew she had consulted, on more than one occasion, with a healer named Don Miguel, a fact he kept secret because of this friar's reputation in the Church as a charlatan and threat. If he now openly invited the friar into his home, he risked his own reputation and backing of the Church. On the other hand, he was haunted by the fear of losing his wife without trying all possibilities. Eventually, his fear won out, and he sent a carriage to bring Don Miguel to his wife.

"Don Miguel came immediately but was greeted by the landowner with a mixture of disdain and hope. He offered to leave the room, as all the other doctors had requested, but Don Miguel insisted he stay in the room, suggesting, in fact, that his participation might be required. Don Miguel went up to the woman, sat on the bed, took both her hands in his, and spoke to her. 'You look absolutely radiant basking in the light that way, Michaela. How are you feeling and what do you want? I know you've wanted to see me, but I couldn't come without your husband's permission.' *My dear Don Miguel, it's true, I've so wanted to see you and have called repeatedly.*'

"'Can she hear you? Is she responding? What does she say?' Nervous excitement completely pushed aside the landowner's arrogance as he danced around Don Miguel searching for clues and answers. He responded by asking Michaela if she wished to speak to her husband, and with her affirmation he told the landowner to take her left hand in his right, and take Don Miguel's right hand in his left. As soon as he did this his whole body literally jumped straight up into the air as though a bolt of lightening had struck him. He immediately heard his wife's voice inside his own head. *My darling Antonio, thank you so much for bringing to me this great healer, and the only man who can save me! I am in tremendous distress. I can no longer exist in my life with you if I cannot express my spirituality openly. If we are truly to flourish together, we must share this part of our lives in an honest and open way. Otherwise we will drift further apart until our marriage exists in name only, which for me is a slow death I refuse to suffer.*'

"The landowner became totally overwhelmed by all this, dropped his head on her abdomen, and began sobbing. Unaccustomed to projecting his thoughts, he spoke out loud to her. 'My dear Michaela, I've been so blinded by my own ambitions. Without you, everything I own has no meaning. Come back and guide me with the help of this great Don Miguel.'

"When he heard her assent Don Miguel prepared her to come back to her body and restored her vitality. She opened her eyes, and the whole room became instantly filled with a bright light as though the window shades had been lifted, although they still remained down. Antonio lifted his head and sat staring into Michaela's face with a paralyzing expression. She took him into her arms; a very transformed man. When they finally looked up they realized they were alone, and Don Miguel had vanished.

"Once again we were back in Carana's office. Father Francesco Buonapedire was still on the floor, but was no longer in the same physical pain. He opened his eyes and very self-consciously pulled himself onto a chair. His demeanor had totally changed. 'What a fool I've been,' he said, voicing his feelings without directing them to anyone of us in particular. 'I'm still deeply in pain, but it's not physical. I feel a great spiritual agony from all the hurt and suffering I've caused others, all to further my own ambition, and believing I acted with the blessings of my religion. Now I know why Don Antonio left the Church. I, too, have to change, but I don't have such an angel for a wife as he does in Michaela to help me. What can I do?'

"'Go tomorrow to see Antonio and Michaela,' Don Miguel responded. 'You will find a friend and comfort in both of them. Be open, honest, and humble with them, and you will receive the support and guidance you are seeking.' Buonapedire got up to leave, then stopped, and began to say something, but nothing came out of his mouth. Instead, he came over and gave each of us a hug, and we could all feel the hardened barriers of a long sealed heart quickly disintegrate and begin to emit a radiant glow.

"Just after Father Buonapedire left another client came in. 'We'll leave you alone with this one,' Rolana said, 'and see you later this evening.' We all bid each other goodbye, and Rolana took us back home. We arrived at the temple and I realized I was hungry again, as well as a bit tired. We took food and resumed our places at the table. 'Well, Narada, a lot of traveling for one day! How do you feel?' I told her how I felt and wondered why I should feel so tired, as I didn't think I had done very much.

"'You did a great deal; actually, much more than you realize. It takes a lot of energy to take the psychic trips we did with Carana and even more energy to materially transport your body. You still are not able to generate the level of energy necessary for such body trips, but it's obvious you've been able to take various psychic trips on your own. Although I supplied the energy needed for us to visit Carana and return, the physical transformation you went through is not something you're accustomed to. The physical body has to go through an adjustment with each transformation, and this takes energy. You've never done this before, and you just made two transformations, requiring two adjustments.'

"'I'm not sure I understand what you mean by having enough energy to undergo these transformations, or even to take these psychic trips,' I asked Rolana.

"'You know more than you realize, Narada, you just forget. In fact you had a poignant experience several years ago in which you yourself realized you didn't have enough energy to move into another dimension.' I sat racking my brains searching the files of my memory to recover what Rolana was suggesting. I couldn't find anything and wondered if she weren't confusing me with someone else. 'No, my dear Narada, I'm not confusing you. Look in the file from the trip you took to the southwest region of your country.'

"All of a sudden I recalled the incident she was referring to. I was visiting various ancient native American sites at the time. One in particular provided me a unique experience. The site was composed of two main sections divided by a protrusion from the ground, like a ridge, that forced the visitor to walk around to get from one side to the other. The first side, which was more directly off the minor road and, therefore, more easily accessible to tourists, was a sink hole that contained on the upper walls of its perimeter the remains of former cliff dwellings—cave-like structures where the local population lived. The stream that ran underground and subsequently created the sink hole, continued to run under the ridge to the other side.

"After I felt I had sufficiently satisfied the curious explorer in me, I walked around the ridge to the other side. I was as delighted as surprised to find the place void of tourists. Being less accessible, most tourists never bothered to inspect it. The difference between the first side and this was amazing. While the first was lifeless and still, this side presented a sharp contrast. The stream that ran through it provided an oasis of verdant and lush foliage all around. It seemed to be teaming with more than just the visible life!

"I sat on a rock along the wall constructed long ago to channel the water and irrigate the fields below. I felt such an incredible sense of peace that I had little difficulty letting the bubbling of the stream and the chirping of the birds totally relax me and allow me to enter a deep meditative state. After a while I became aware that I was sitting in the middle of what I could only describe as a resort, or health spa. The amazing part of it, however, is that all its inhabitants were disembodied! I remember going up to the 'entrance' of their resort, looking in, and seeing all these 'light bodies' or 'entities' socializing and having fun. I wanted to go in, but wasn't able to, and realized at the time that I just wasn't able to generate the energy necessary for moving into their dimension.

"I guess I had forgotten because after that experience and after I had returned home, the event began to seem more like the product of a fanciful imagination, and I let it go. Not until Rolana referred to it did I accept that it had indeed occurred. She said that many people have experiences all the time that seem extraordinary, but since they have no framework or context in which to place them, they believe the events were produced by an overactive imagination or the result of taking some medication. While this may also be the case, more often than not the experiences are real, in the sense that those individuals truly tap into other non-material dimensions of life. Out of fear that family and friends may think they've gone slightly off their rockers, they often keep such experiences secret, push them back into the recesses of their minds, and try to forget them.

"'You've already seen, Narada, how you have received energy from us that enables you to do more things. This is a natural phenomenon that occurs between people all the time, although they often don't recognize it. Someone may not be feeling very energetic but then springs to life because of the arrival of a special friend, for example. It's important to keep in mind, however, that energy exchanges go both ways. A person can be feeling very lively and ready to party when someone comes along, and by something as small as a gesture or a remark, instantly causes that liveliness to crumble. This is why it becomes so important to learn to become vigilant about our own energy fields and about those around that have an impact on us. Our spiritual practices and exercises that work with our breath, body, and energy, help us develop the awareness and control necessary to move into higher conscious states and dimensions.'

"By this point my fatigue began to overwhelm me. Rolana suggested I take a short rest before the evening came when the rest of our family would join us. I heartily assented so I could be as present and alert as possible when we were all gathered. Later that evening Carana joked again about all the traveling I had done that day. He turned to Balcano and asked, 'Professor, are you going to be taking Narada on any trips tomorrow?' 'Well, maybe some inner mind journeys,' Balcano responded, as a sense of mystery and intrigue played about the lines of his face. This little exchange raised several questions in my head. I was about to put them out when Rolana immediately followed with an account of the adventures of Father Francesco Buonapedire. No other opportunity that evening ever presented itself for raising my questions, but I was content to leave them for the next day.

Chapter Seven

The Professor

"The next morning I went to the temple knowing Balcano was going to be my teacher that day. I had been looking forward to being with him and was glad finally to have that opportunity. He always acted the merry maker, telling jokes and stories, which made me wonder why he was called the professor. I figured the title was everyone else's way of joking about his fun-loving nature. I thought I'd find him at the dinner table, but as I didn't see him there, or anywhere else in the building, I just sat down and started to eat, expecting him to pop in eventually. That was sooner than I thought. I hadn't even swallowed the food I had just put into my mouth when he literally popped up right across from me at the table, wearing a big, red clown's nose! My surprise was enough to make me jettison the food right out my mouth and splatter him on the face. At that point the two of us burst into laughter, fell on the floor, and rolled around in fits of hilarity.

"'So, you're wondering why they call me the professor?' Balcano finally asked me after we settled down. 'I used to be a professor in a former lifetime, for one reason, but the appellation didn't appear until I began the role of guide/master/teacher/guru, whatever you wish to call it, at various spiritual retreat centers throughout the world. I currently *hold court* at five such centers, so you can imagine how busy that keeps me, popping in here, popping in there; students and so-called aspirants constantly making demands and pleading their hopes and desires for greater spiritual attainment while unwilling to engage in any serious discipline. Not all, of course. Some are actually quite advanced, and one day may work with you.'

"If I were unprepared for this explanation of Balcano's background after the way he greeted me, the serious discussion he then launched into proved a major contrast. It was obvious that his fun-loving nature set in stark relief his enjoyment of exploring, discussing, and teaching about inner mind states and other esoteric topics. It also became obvious the way he enjoyed quick transitions.

"'We are born from an inner state of being and go forth into the universe until we arrive at the place we started from. We only know the extent of this depending on the extent we go back inside to our original state, to know who we truly are. The extent to which we can expand into the universe depends on how far back we've been able to go to the Source—our origin. The moment we've gone from one end to the other, the ends cease to exist, and we merge with the Source.'

"I was completely unprepared for this, and I'm sure my bewilderment was communicated in more than one way. He responded appropriately with some explanation.

"'You see, Narada, some people, especially in modern western society, believe and act as though the world revolves around them. From their mechanistic understanding of the universe, they believe they come into existence as the result of some biological operation that forms a body that allows them to perform all kinds of things. They can do these things because they also have a brain, which they think acts like a computer to regulate the body and generate thoughts and ideas, which the body then carries out. Since they believe they came into existence as a result of a biological process—which is physical in nature—then their identity tends to become entrenched in and inseparable from their physical body and physical existence. In actuality, each one of us exists prior to the creation of each mind and body.

"'Greater than our mind and body, we are born of a Mind that is, along with its own body, the creation of an even greater Mind. At the first level of Mind, we give birth to our current mind and body. At the next level of Mind we give birth to the stream of lives we acquire in each of our successive lives. There are infinite levels of Mind and the bodies they create. Many religious teachings insist that there is a finite number of such levels, and the number varies widely. To fix a number, however, is to lock us into what most people believe is the only mind and body they have. In the notion of the infinite we are pulled into an ever expanding consciousness. As we do this we are both more capable of conceiving an ever greater cosmos, as well as the Consciousness whose creation it all is.

"'So when I say that we are born from an inner state of being, I mean that the next level of Mind—the one existing prior to our physical mind and body—*sends out* the intelligence, if you will, that enables its soul to be outfitted with a new body of flesh, with the components necessary to make it appear self-sustaining and self-governing. The body that then seemingly *comes together* or develops as a result of the mechanistic DNA process described in cell biology is really just one very small part of our total being. Since it is the only part that can be observed by its physical senses, people come to believe it's our only reality. We can not perceive any higher levels of being with any of the *equipment* of a lower level mind and body. In other words, nothing in the structure of the physical mind or body allows us to perceive even our next level of Mind, the one that created each physical body. Which is not to say, of course, that we can't do it. It does mean that while the mind's intellect may not be directly capable of such perception, it is capable of directing us to read, contemplate, and study the esoteric teachings and sacred writings of people who have experienced higher states of consciousness and can articulate them and reflect their wisdom back to the reader. The intellect can then direct us to engage in the best body exercises and physical practices that, together with the work of the intellect, the Mind of our creation then has an opening in our awareness to become evident.'

"'I'm not sure I'm really getting all of this, Balcano.'

"'You see, Narada, the problem is that you think you must understand this intellectually, that is, as the result of the processes of your mind. As I pointed out, however, all the intellect can do is to direct us along the path that, along with its body, promotes those conditions for awareness to emerge. In fact you already do understand exactly what I'm discussing, but you only know that when you have stepped out of the confines and limitations of the mind and its intellect. Once you have done this, then you can experience your higher Mind directly. This process is more difficult for some cultures than others, because different cultures socialize their people to experience the world differently. Each culture has a predominant world view, or construct of its reality and how to interact with it. Each new member of that culture becomes educated and socialized into its society's dominant construct of reality. By the time that member has reached adulthood his reality construct, if it was never challenged, has become so entrenched in his mind that often there is little or no room for even contemplating the possibility of the existence of other constructs of reality.

"'Each social construct allows its society to develop in a particular manner. A society, like our contemporary western world, put greater emphasis on the development of the intellect. While its resulting achievements in the material world are extraordinary, the costs of such accomplishments have been high. We have an example of this in the inability many people exhibit in relating to nature in a caring, loving, and nurturing way. When people can't connect with a part of themselves, they cannot connect with that part in others. To the extent people have highly developed their intellect, and neglected their bodies, emotions, and the soul, they cannot connect with the bodies, emotions, and souls of others.

"'The reality construct of some other cultures puts less emphasis on the development of the intellect to the exclusion of its other component parts. Its members more easily integrate the body, intellect, emotions and soul. For them it becomes easier to leave open, or create, a space in which higher Mind can be observed and learned from. These people don't have to go through the same process that many others from the modern industrialized world do in order to attain higher spiritual and conscious awareness. They don't have to, for example, begin a hunt for the best readings to contemplate, the right spiritual exercise to practice, or the one true master to guide them. That's because they're already doing those things; they're built into the very fabric of their social construct.'

"'What did you mean, Balcano, when you said we go forth into the universe until we arrive at the place we started from?'

"'I mean that Formless Consciousness, in its Unmanifested State, is our origin. As It manifests It creates a level of Mind, which in turn gives birth to another level of Mind, and on and on until it arrives at the level of the mind and body we know as our self identify. This mind is far removed from its next higher level of Mind, though only in its thinking process. When the individual engages in those practices that allow its next higher level of Mind to be contemplated and accepted, then the individual has begun the process of going forth into the universe. That is because with the awareness that each higher level of Mind brings, much more of the universe can be embraced. That is the feeling of expansiveness that you and many others experience when you allow yourselves to enter higher levels of Mind. Eventually, the individual arrives at the Place he started from, which is Formless Consciousness Itself.

"'This concept is extremely important as it concerns our ability to create. The more deeply we *know* higher Minds, the greater ability we have to create from any one of those levels. If we combine that with the discipline to be able to focus, then we really have a very powerful means for manifesting on the physical plane whatever we want. The operation of the bow and arrow is illustrative. The more you can pull the arrow back, the greater force it has to go forward and farther. If, however, you lack in discipline, then you won't practice enough to develop your skills and won't exercise enough to develop your strength. As a result you won't be able to control the force at the level you're pulling the arrow back. The obvious result of this situation is that at any moment the arrow will just slip out of your hands and fly off in any direction, possibly with grave consequences. Similarly it is not sufficient just to be able to attain high states of consciousness and access deeper levels of Mind. In fact, as you can understand with the example of the bow and arrow, it may be dangerous. The discipline we bring to our evolving spiritual development is crucial.

"'So, when people believe they come into existence solely as the result of a physical biological process, they greatly limit themselves to the knowledge and awareness of which their physical part is capable. As a result, they are not capable of truly understanding—and sometimes even accepting—the awareness and experiences that other people have as a result of having opened up to higher Mind. People operating from the limitations of mind may deny the validity of knowledge and experience others get from their contact with a higher Mind. That is to be expected, because higher Mind must be experienced directly. The mind's intellect can then try and make sense of the reality of higher Mind and higher consciousness and then describe and articulate it for others, thus providing a kind of map that helps guide others toward their own direct experiences.'

"'Balcano, I'm not sure I understand what you meant when you said that at the next level of Mind we give birth to the stream of lives described by each of our successive lives.'

"'A stream of lives includes all the multiple and successive incarnations of a soul; each mind and body that the Mind creates.

Each new incarnation is a vibrational impulse of its next higher level of Mind. That level of Mind continues to emit such impulses until the consciousness of an individual mind finally and eventually opens up to its higher, birthing Mind. Each incarnation, therefore, is a unique and invaluable opportunity to transcend the limitations of its physical existence by discovering and opening up to its higher Mind. Fortunately we don't have to start from scratch with each new incarnation. While we do begin each incarnation with a new body, mind, and intellect, the soul of each particular life stream contains all the impressions, knowledge, and memory created by all the other incarnations of its stream. This helps explain why people get those feelings that a person they meet, or a place they visit, seems so familiar. Such familiarity is caused by impressions of their soul that *leak through* the barriers of their mind and body. It can be disturbing because people feel they can't quite "put their finger on it," can't quite remember, but they, nevertheless, maintain a nagging sense somewhere in their being that they know a particular person or place.

"'In fact, it is the make-up of our souls that helps explain the conditions and events we experience in each incarnation. The phenomenon is described by the word *karma*, and people have known about it for thousands of years. It describes in part that vast storage of impressions, knowledge, and memory that coalesce into the impulses from which the Mind conceives itself back into physical form again.'

"I started to feel as though I needed a break to process all these ideas Balcano was presenting to me. He noticed my energy level shift and suggested we take a meditation break, as a way of re-energizing and centering myself. He instructed me on some breathing techniques and conducted a guided meditation involving the *chakras*. The word chakra is an ancient Sanskrit word that has come into increasingly common parlance in the western world in the past several decades. It means rotating disk, or wheel, and refers to the numerous force centers that exist all throughout the physical body, but are generally seen as part of the more subtle bodies that interpenetrate the physical one. While there are over a hundred chakras located in various places in the body, most people typically refer to the seven major ones located along the spine from the base to the top of the head and facing front and back. They are integral to the system whereby the vital life force—known as *Prana* in Sanskrit, or *Chi* in Chinese— vitalizes the systems and organs of the physical body. Their development is also integral to the higher states of consciousness people can experience, as well as the various powers of greater sense perception some people demonstrate.

"Before we began the meditation, however, Balcano suggested we move to the other end of the temple, behind the altar. I had seen this area before, and while I was curious, I never ventured into it. It was actually a fairly large area, one that could accommodate our whole group, although it was constructed in such a way that the space seemed just right regardless of how many people were there. Moreover the space contained a powerful energy field that you could feel as soon as you stepped into it; similar to what you might experience walking into a very holy place, only stronger.

"'You must be careful of your thoughts while in here,' Balcano warned me, 'because the energy field, vibrating at a very high rate, will take anything generated here—including thoughts and feelings—then focus and send it amplified into the universe. Now that you've centered yourself and become comfortable, I want you to focus all your attention on your root chakra. Feel it as it breathes; its impulses. Feel its deep and rooted connection down into the earth. Now slowly feel that energy move up into the sacral chakra, and like the first, feel it pulsating with the energy, becoming increasingly vibrant as you bring more energy into it. Continue that process slowly up through all your chakras, allowing the focus of your attention to bring the energy up from the previous chakra. You feel each one in turn becoming vibrant and radiant. When you reach your crown chakra, feel the energy continue up infinitely into space. Let that energy go as it will, then repeat the process, feeling it enter into your base chakra and move up. Continue repeating this process until you feel a steady flow of energy streaming into your base chakra, traveling up, and vitalizing each chakra in turn with more and more energy.

"'Now let's take a little stroll into inner space. Imagine yourself walking down a path alongside a huge forest. Many people don't like to go in there because they say it's a mysterious and foreboding place. It seems very inviting from the outside, however, and you decide to enter. Just as you make your decision, a pathway into it magically seems to appear. You appreciate your luck, and begin the journey, becoming more joyous with each step as you realize how incredibly beautiful and exquisite it really is. In fact, you wonder why you had never wanted to come in before. Along the way you hear the sounds of birds, as you might expect, but these sing a song more delightful and delicate than you've ever heard. Then, through the rustling of the trees, whose leaves emit the sweet sounds of satisfaction they receive from the gossamer breeze massaging them, comes another expression of God's joy. You listen closely to determine its direction, then carefully make your way there, always alert not to lose the trail. As the sound gets louder and you know you're real close, an opening in the brush reveals a rivulet, whose bubbling chimes were the charm that enticed you to come and sample its sweet freshness. When you bend down to do so, you see yourself.

"'What you see is not your reflection, however, it is you, your life. Like the numerous other rivulets, this one, too, will feed into the larger stream of your lives. This, like the water in countless other streams and tributaries will feed the rivers that flow into the great ocean of Supreme and Formless Consciousness, only to be returned to the sky, condense, and fall down to earth to begin again.

"'The massive trees you walked past stand like great pillars in the majestic temple of the forest and sink their anchoring roots deep into the earth, where they draw the nutrition that enables them to spread out their limbs, branches, twigs, and leaves, that regularly drop to the ground, disintegrate, and nourish the trees for their continued growth. In the disintegration of Its matter, the Life Force is actually manifesting Its creative nature, as the disintegration of matter then creates the conditions for further growth. So, too, in the disintegration and death of the physical body, the soul is similarly nourished, and the nutriments for its subsequent lifetimes are laid down, hence to influence the direction, conditions, and forms of its subsequent lives.

"'Some cultures and people in the world and throughout history have understood and celebrated this process, knowing how it renews and strengthens their community. Many other people, however, fear and push it away. This is understandable. The ego has a natural repulsion to things in disintegration, because they remind it of its own demise, while it struggles fiercely to hold onto its identity—its mind and body. Not until we locate the stream of our lives and find our own life in it will we be free of that fear. Not until the determined attachment of the ego is transcended can we achieve the freedom that transcends the limitations of physical existence. Our bodies are not the obstacle; rather, it is the ego's insistent desire to maintain consciousness at the level of its mind and body.'

"Whether it was Balcano's resonant voice, the inherent energy of our meditation spot, his powerful chakra exercise, or all three, I wasn't sure. But before he even got to his guided meditation, I was already in another dimension, another state of consciousness. I had expanded into an ocean of much greater consciousness and saw not only the stream that included Narada's life, but infinitely more as well. My normal set of boundaries ceased to exist, and I expanded into a formless field unbounded by time and space as most people know it. What I *knew* during that experience I could never adequately articulate in words. I could only hope that, like the poet whose exquisite description of the most sublime love invites readers to discover the feeling for themselves, others would similarly seek the *knowing* that transcends their own mind and body consciousness.

"I don't know how much time had elapsed since Balcano stopped talking. When I became aware of it, I looked over and saw him surrounded by a luminous egg of golden, radiant, and shimmering light. 'If you looked at a mirror, Narada, you would see the same luminous egg around you,' he then said. We stayed like that for quite some time, when Balcano suggested we move back to our former spot. That was fine with me, as I wished to ask him a question I had had for several days.

"'Balcano, during my first day here, Carana mentioned the inherent power of gold and silver that you all had just discovered before the Spanish conquerors came. I had expected him to elaborate on that, but he moved onto other things. Can you tell me more about that?'

"'Ah, Narada, an excellent question! For many cultures throughout history, the sun was considered to be a symbol of male energy, while the moon, a symbol of the female energy. Although some ancient societies saw the sun as the embodiment of the female goddess, this belief system eventually lost ground to the more predominant association to a god. Both the male and female energies are inherent in every human being and are distinguished by different qualities. It is perhaps unfortunate that so many cultures throughout history, and predominantly today, have so separated these energies and identified their respective qualities as exclusively belonging to one sex or the other. That is, they believe that what is typically considered as male energy is solely descriptive of men and as female, only of women. The fact is that we achieve greater wholeness to the extent we, as individuals, can develop and embody within ourselves the strength of both the male and female. This is often what couples seek to do—though largely unconsciously—through their relationships.

"'Gold, for obvious reasons, has long been held as the symbol of the sun. Its many qualities, such as color, brightness, durability, and immortality, suggest the sun. In fact, the science of alchemy used the same symbol for both the sun and gold. Silver, with its shimmering, water-like quality, has similarly had a long symbolic association with the moon. These metals, therefore, have not only been prized by many for their intrinsic value, but as well for the various qualities associated with them.

"'Alchemy is the juncture where the qualities associated with the male and female energies, and high spiritual attainment come together. There is an innate, driving force within all people that seeks to get us to transcend each individual ego and the boundaries and limitations associated with it. While this force derives from the higher Mind—our greater birth essence—it is very difficult for humans to overcome the force of their own karmic creations, and the power of their attractions and repulsions. This sets up an existential conflict in us: The expression of ourselves through the actions of the ego, versus the search for, and expression of, that essence of ourselves that transcends the ego. Because the resolution of this conflict is a long and arduous process, requiring the disciplined mind and body that is attained only after extensive and dedicated practice, people have often sought short-cuts. This explains, in part, the use of drugs—including, in some people, alcohol—and other substances, especially those that help induce in them altered states of mind and consciousness.

"'Alchemy was another method expected to bring riches to the individual who practiced the science and art. As with many other things in life, this too had its baser, as well as finer sides, or, to put it another way, its material and spiritual aspects. Materially, the practitioner sought wealth through the transformation of baser metals into gold. Spiritually the practitioner sought the transformation of baser qualities of physical existence into spiritual awareness, and the transcendence of limitations that physical existence imposed on them. In its spiritual aspects, alchemy is symbolic of our inner unfolding, the transformations of our emotions and values.

"'Love is a good example of this. The development of our capacity to express unconditional and non-judgmental love from that which is limited and conditional can be represented by the alchemical transformation of baser metals into gold. Like gold the love that is an expression of higher and purer Mind cannot be contaminated or destroyed. This love is immortal, untarnished, and infinite. As it is complete within itself, it seeks nothing in return, yet it reflects the bright and pure essence of the universe. Like the purity of gold, this love is not contaminated by the material and selfish desires that accompany lower, conditional love.

"'As gold and silver came increasingly to be associated both with the male and female energies, as well as the awareness of higher spiritual states, this increased their abilities for creating harm, as well as good. We've already seen how such substances throughout history have excited the rapacious appetites of conquerors and thieves. Its beneficial qualities have been their ability to help develop and balance the male and female energies within people, and hence promote their greater spiritual attainment. This was the hidden potential that Carana spoke about your first evening with us. We were still calculating the proper quantities and conditions so that our gold and silver could have been used to develop greater balance and harmony among our people when the Conquistadors came to our shores. You know from the account Carana gave your first evening with us what followed after their arrival. We realized that if we could imbue a certain amount of gold and silver with the right elemental, then those amounts would have the power to influence the remaining gold and silver scattered throughout the world.'

"'What do you mean by imbuing them with the right elemental?' I asked Balcano.

"'Simply put *elementals* are forms that have been created from our thoughts. Our thoughts are more real and powerful than most people realize. Every thought that we conceive is an energetic vibration that takes on a body of elementals, which is a basic building block of matter, a more immediate manifestation of Vital Life Force. In fact, it is precisely this human capability to create that is behind the meaning of the notion that people were created in the image of God. Just as higher Mind sends out the

Thought to create an individual, so do individuals, in turn, have the ability to manifest their own creations by sending out thoughts. The great difference, however, is power, focus, and intent.

"'People generally go through the day generating thousands and thousands of thoughts, a steady stream of generally unconnected, and often incompletely formulated thoughts. As each thought goes out a form is created by the essence of those elementals that get attached to it. The life of this form, however, depends on the amount and power of thought that created it. Most of them are weak and short lived because little thought power went into them. Higher Minds, capable of powerful, focused and sustained thoughts, can easily manifest instantly into physical existence whatever they want. Most people, due to lack of mental discipline, are not capable of focusing and sustaining a thought necessary for instant manifestation. Usually it takes them a long period of time, as discouragement and negativity weaken the originally intended thought, and may even eventually abort or alter it.

"'A particular thought form is strengthened each time a thought similar to the one that created it is sent out. You can easily see how a thought form can become very powerful if not just one person, but many, continue to send out the same thought. If this event continued for some period of time, a thought form could easily become a very strong entity with the power to influence others. This, in fact, is the situation that exists in the world today. You can probably think of many objects or ideas that have excited people's imaginations to such an extent and for so long, that the particular object or idea has taken on a life of its own, and the mere mention of it instantly generates a mood, feeling, or desire that's strongly charged with emotion. What we're concerned with here is a perfect example of this. A slight reference to gold and silver can quickly excite the passions in some people.

"'So our intent with the quantities of gold and silver that our rulers had stored was twofold, or rather to imbue them with two thought forms that would then begin to affect people differently. The first would work on neutralizing the material desire, longing, and greed that had become so powerful as a result of the countless thoughts generated throughout the ages about those metals. The second was to strengthen them with the already associated thought forms of the higher qualities of the male and female energies, which would, in turn, help promote and balance those qualities within each individual.

"'Our plans to do this were, of course, halted by the invasion. If we had been able to carry them out, however, we calculated that the energy generated by this mass would positively affect the remaining gold and silver in the world through vibrational resonance. This would then have promoted the general spiritual development of people throughout the world, as well as lessened the destructive power influenced by these metals.'

"Balcano suddenly stopped talking. I looked up and saw him gazing at the sky, his eyes fixated on a point seemingly beyond the galaxy. Like a searchlight blazing against the deep blue of the late afternoon sky, a ray of light emanated from the center of his forehead, and accompanied his gaze as though it were lighting his way. He slowly turned his head in my direction until his beam fully illuminated my face. I was as frightened as I was mesmerized. With a force greater than a powerful magnet, his light took possession of my gaze. The light was unlike anything I had ever seen. Pulsating beads of brilliance emanated from the center and spiraled around like a vortex. It rotated faster and faster, until the outlines around Balcano's body started to get faint. Slowly his whole body turned into an amorphous mass, like a cloud, and as it did so the vortex of light diminished and disappeared. I remained riveted to my spot with unbelieving eyes and unable to turn away. After a short time, the cloud began to condense, but not to become Balcano.

"Where Balcano had just sat across from me now stood a huge and majestic condor. I shook my head trying to fathom what I had just seen. He beckoned me with his commanding beak, then took off in flight, forming circles close to the ground that extended further and further out, allowing me to follow him. My extended steps quickly turned into a run across the meadow, faster and faster trying to keep up with him. I ran and ran, until just at the point I thought I was going to collapse, I realized I was no longer treading earth. I had fallen into some sort of shaft. The light from above soon disappeared and I dropped through the darkness with increasing speed. After what felt like an eternity, I realized I was no longer falling, but held still, as though cushioned by an air pillow. Yet the air swirled around me with the swiftness of a tornado. All of a sudden it seemed as though someone had pulled the air pillow from under me, but I didn't resume falling as before. Instead, I felt an inner force pulling on me with an accelerating power as though it were propelling me through the very boundaries of physical existence. I have no idea how long this lasted. After some time, however, I began to experience physical changes, as though my body were turning into someone else. I couldn't see anything as I was still held fast within the cocoon of darkness. Soon everything began to change. As the whirlwind around me slowly diminished, so, too, the darkness dissipated.

"I found myself standing inside a lush, tropical garden, embellished with pools of water and statues of saints and mystics. It seemed as though I were surrounded by an eternity of serenity. The air had an unknown fragrance that seemed to heal the body as much as the soul. The birds sang as though they were serenading the angels. A refreshing mist cooled my skin as a warm breeze gently rustled the leaves. The breeze also stirred my clothes, and as my eye caught the flowing movement of material, I looked down to find myself wrapped in a loose-fitting garment of silk adorned with a pattern of unmistakable exotic Indian art. My amazement now altered with alarm, I rushed to a pool to examine my reflection. My face was not as I had known it, and I furiously inspected myself further.

"All of a sudden, seemingly out of nowhere, a giant black condor came swooping down out of the sky and landed just feet from where I stood. I stared at it in astonishment. Finally, as though compelled by its own curiosity, a voice broke through my silence. 'Bal-cano?' I called out haltingly. As if just waiting to be addressed, he slowly disassembled his bird form, once again to emerge the Balcano I knew.

"'Well, Narada, how was your trip? I see you've arrived fully intact. I, myself, prefer to fly Condor Express.'

"I was fortunately next to a bench and sank into it with a weight of confusion and bewilderment upon me. As I couldn't sort through all my questions, I remained silent. Balcano suggested we stroll through the gardens and came over to assist me. He wondered if nothing touched my memory, yet it was that very thing that fueled my turmoil. Everything seemed so familiar, so natural, yet with so many pieces in place, I still couldn't figure out the picture.

"'Don't you recognize the ashram you created, Narada? Or, perhaps I should address you as Sri Sankara?'

"The mere mention of that name and his question sent a vibration that reverberated down to the core of my being. I realized I was Sankara, as much as I was Narada, and as much as I was Winston.

"'This was the identity you assumed in your rebirth subsequent to your departure from us after that horrific blast high in the Andes. Your *performance* here was magnificent! Your whole life was devoted to the service of the Divine Goddess and to sharing that devotion with others. Toward that end you created this sublime center that you presided over as head priestess. In fact you asked for and received my help in setting it up. I came periodically as guest guru, you might say, and stayed on to provide spiritual guidance to your following after you gave up this identity. I told you earlier that I was the spiritual leader at various retreat centers around the world. Well, this is one of them. I have been coming here now for over two hundred years, periodically changing my appearance for those who remain stuck in the illusions of the physical plane.'

"'How did I come to incarnate as Sankara, and why did you bring me here now?'

"'One of the things you still had to cultivate, and which we were working on when you left us, was the full expression and development of your female energy and power. This was the perfect opportunity for it. The main thing that remained after that, which you are doing now in your current lifetime, is the complete integration of the highest aspects of both the male and female energies. I brought you here figuring that your remembering this lifetime as priestess would facilitate this integration.'

"'It's not uncommon then, Balcano, for people to change genders from one lifetime to the next?'

"'This is thinking that comes from identification with the ego and the physical plane of existence. Gender, as well as all the other physical traits people commonly use to define themselves, are only aspects of the body that the soul happens to be fleshed out in throughout one particular lifetime. How can you truly say you are Winston, if you are also Sankara, Narada, and all those others before Narada? The experience of being a woman can be vastly different from that of being a man depending on the society one lives in. Similarly other major traits that are commonly used to distinguish and to discriminate people may engender vastly different lives. These differences are largely brought about by each person's own individual karma, as well as the karma formed by the various groups and communities an individual is associated with. The lessons we need in order to grow into the complete wholeness of ourselves are custom made. And lessons cannot be skipped either. There is no complete wholeness with pieces missing. You undoubtedly know people who go through the same type of trial time and time again, who experience the same mishap repeatedly. These people are not learning what they need to from their experiences. Until they do, they'll just keep repeating them.

"'We should now return to the future, Narada. The reason you're in the garden at the moment as Sankara is you are preparing your thoughts for a talk you are giving tonight to a large, visiting group. This is the first direct connection you had with your subsequent lifetime as Winston. I will come back to Sankara to explain things further to her.'

"We then went back to the Andes and to my current lifetime. We returned the same way, although this time I didn't have to run after Balcano the Condor. Instead he instructed me to take up my lotus meditation position at a special place in the garden reserved solely for my use and enter into a deep inner space beyond the confines of the ego. Then I experienced much the same sensations I did on the out-bound flight. Balcano explained to me that this type of travel to other time zones and other lifetimes is much more difficult than the type of trips I took to visit Carana. It requires much more energy as the barriers that have to be crossed are much more formidable. Furthermore it can be dangerous and should not be attempted in the beginning without the guidance of a master. I had no trouble with that, as I had absolutely no idea what to do anyway. Balcano said that was true for now, but would eventually change. He also said such travel gets easier and easier when the individual develops greater facility in manipulating the subatomic structure of physical matter.

"It was late in the day when we got back, and we would all be assembling soon for our evening get-together. Nevertheless, while I was still with Balcano, and a question still loomed in my mind from an earlier talk with Carana, I decided now was the best time to address it. I wondered why we had been known as the *Group of the Esoteric*.

"'This was not an official name, of course, Narada, but rather an informal designation that arose during a conversation between a number of us and some in the larger religious body. It was a reference one of them used in a cynical attempt to discredit us because we were not engaged in the day-to-day operations of ministering to the flock, which they prided themselves as being of supreme importance. While the word was meant to put us down, it actually served as an accurate distinction between our two groups and consequently stuck. Yet while they labeled us as esoteric, they couldn't see themselves as being described by its opposite, or exoteric. That's because they believed themselves to be such great experts of the religious texts. And compared to everybody else they were, because few others had access to any of the sacred writings, or could even read in those languages to understand them.

"'Exoteric refers to the external, the outer; essentially that which is the manifestation of Supreme Spirit. In the religious sense, it includes the rituals, rules and regulations by which people are to be guided in the course of their lives. For many people it is desirous to have a set of guidelines that enables them to steer the course of their lives; a set of values directing their behavior. Life is undoubtedly very difficult and full of competing demands, conflicts, yearnings, desires, and powerful forces pulling people apart. Although initially useful and helpful tools for commandeering these myriad forces, while the focus of religion remains with the exoteric, the people under such guidance may be hindered in their inner search; the search that leads them to discover the essence of all outer manifestation.

"'This is the search that emphasis on the esoteric leads to. This is an inner search, a journey inside one's being back to the origin of one's soul. This is the search that guides people toward their commonality, their shared essence; what unites them in the awareness that they are all creations of the One Spirit. By contrast the exoteric that is of great concern to many religious people emphasizes the outer form and by its nature its differences with other outer forms. How many people throughout history have been motivated to kill and destroy in the name of their religion? Like the web spiders create to trap their prey, the religious dogma some religious leaders focus on hangs as an illusory web to ensnare the faithful. To destroy others because they have created different religious forms is like bombing a mirage. Supreme Spirit is neither destroyed or created, but rather, manifests Itself in infinitely different and ever-changing forms.

"'The twelve of us were content to work in harmony with our religious brothers and sisters, but motivated by jealously and ambition, some of their leaders sought to destroy us. Each of us had a unique role to play, one that recognized the numerous and vastly different levels of awareness driving each individual. And this is as true today as it was then. As a result, what is right for one person is unnecessary for another. Each individual has at the moment distinct lessons to learn and is ready to advance to a different rung on the infinite ladder that leads toward Supreme awareness. These rungs must be advanced one by one, and when artificially jumped over by forced or induced means, the person runs a risk of slipping and falling; perhaps fatally. When advanced in the proper order unique to each individual, the strength and awareness gained from moving to the next rung is sufficient to allow the person to engage the next lesson, and hence, attain the next rung.

"'No judgment can be assessed to the position of a single rung when viewed from the perspective of inner awareness. At each rung every individual is reflecting a unique facet of Supreme Spirit's Pure Diamond Consciousness. And after we reach for the hand from someone on the rung above us, we can extend a hand to the one just below. In other words, each person is uniquely qualified to help another, and regardless of where each rung lies on the great ladder, all unconditional help that truly assists others is equal.'

"I had so much to think about at that point from my day with Balcano, but little time then to do it. He had no sooner finished speaking when the sounds of revelry announced the arrival of family members. I delighted in the change of pace and intensity this afforded me and felt my soul relax from the unconditional love that massaged it. Later that night, as usual, I sought my sleep before all others and wondered if they ever slept at all. Nevertheless I never felt I was parting with their company and missing something. I felt so connected with every one of them that it seemed they were with me wherever I went. I went to my bed with love in my heart and serenity in my soul, and slumber embraced me as a mother cradling her child."

Chapter Eight

Healing

"The next day was so bizarre. I seemed to transcend from the dreaming to the waking state without ever waking up in the normal sense. It began in the middle of a dream when Zarmano approached me. I had remained intrigued by the healing Manora and Arzano had done days before on me. In the dream Zarmano told me that such healings only seemed extraordinary in the linear, cause/effect, and material model of the universe that most people generally subscribed to. He invited me to visit Andora who was chief healer and supervisor at a healing clinic and retreat center.

"She was expecting us and greeted me warmly. She was in her private study when we arrived and offered to show me around *the estate*, as it was commonly referred to by those who knew of its existence. In fact there was a mystery about this place. It was not advertised, and actually, no one knew its exact location. The reason is that people did not go there of their own accord, but rather, were invited. If they accepted the invitation, it was Zarmano's job to bring them. He brought people from all over the world. It was clear to these patients, who naturally encountered one another, that they came from diverse places, but none of them knew exactly where they had come to, only that they were on the estate. The length of each person's stay was as varied as their particular conditions, but one thing they had in common was that each became transformed by the experience. It was not uncommon, in fact, for strong bonds to be formed among them, and deep friendships were subsequently built around the experience.

"I asked Zarmano how people heard about the place and how he got in contact with them in order to bring them there. He told me that as some people move along the path of their spiritual evolution they not uncommonly encounter a roadblock of such proportions that any further advance seems completely untenable. Turning back is no longer an option, and nothing in their prior conscious experiences provides an answer. The search this engenders often brings about a disaster to their physical being, and they find themselves crushed by the weight of both crises. What they then feel as being the lowest point in their lives often proves the most valuable. Out of the void of their helplessness comes a cry so low, yet so powerful, that its vibration reverberates on Zarmano's consciousness.

"'When I hear such anguished cries,' Zarmano explained further, 'I don't just rush in, sweep people off their feet, and bring them here. In reality people come here when they're ready and ask.'

"'Ready for what?' I asked.

"'Yes! That is the crucial question! Are they truly ready for transformation? Are they ready to heal into greater awareness, into more of their wholeness? Growing into greater awareness is a transformative process, in which the individual's psychic structure becomes rearranged. After such an event the world is viewed as from a different set of eyes. After such an event the individual can't go back and behold the world as before. And with each transformation one expands into greater and greater wholeness, each time enlarging the boundaries that previously defined the limitations of his or her being.

"'So, each call I receive does not evoke from me the same response. I must admit to being occasionally fooled by the extraordinary stubbornness of some people; those who in spite of suffering the gravest of misfortunes refuse to be transformed and seek instead to return to the way of life they had previously maintained. They find in their boundaries, as limiting as they may be, a comfort born of familiarity. Some people cling very tenaciously to their worn patterns, and on the torn fibers of their lives' fabrics they hang the metals of stubbornness—trophies gathered from lost battles. In other words, some people, despite the enormity of the misfortunes that befall them, resist the invitation engendered by illness and other painful situations.'

"'What do you mean by invitation, Zarmano?'

"'Think of it as a way you can use to look at such events to make them easier to deal with; to invest them with some meaning so they don't appear as some random act visiting upon some unsuspecting victim. The very act of doing this brings an immediate advantage: it turns the disempowering disposition of victimization into the empowering position of beneficiary. One is invited to take advantage of the opportunity to grow into the greater wholeness of oneself; to become more aware. But, of course, not everyone accepts the invitation. And, just like an invitation to a social event, this one, too, requires you to go to it. And arriving still isn't enough. You then must actively work at it to make it successful. You must become fully engaged with the process. You must allow yourself to become vulnerable; to step back from your own self and take inventory. You must ask just what constitutes your being and be willing to let go of those things that are going to impede the healing process. You must seek to know those things you shroud in denial. You must be willing to accept that perhaps not everything in your life is working for you and allow yourself to open up to a greater way of being; a life of greater freedom; more whole and more expansive.

"'These are the things I wait for and listen to before bringing someone here. It is very important when bringing healing energy to someone that we are sensitive to their karmic history. This means we should not try to heal someone for our own ego gratification. People often have the need, and even karmic requirement, to move through the pain and suffering caused by their particular situation. Simply removing the causative agent of their suffering may mean removing the means by which they need to move through the forces of their own karma, as well as any particular lessons they need to learn as a result of dealing with their trial.

"'Once we realize this we can provide whatever healing energy we are capable of, then step back, and let go of the outcome. I say *we*, because in actuality, every person is capable of providing healing energy. It is not something we command with our egos, or something dictated by the brain, but rather the energy of divine love we channel through our hearts simply by opening up to it. That's because this energy is naturally healing. It seeks to bring back into a state of balance and harmony any situation or condition where it's directed. It is the creative force of Supreme Consciousness that human beings, endowed with our free will, can either work with or against. Although it operates from a much greater intelligence we can easily interfere with its operation by injecting our own notion of what the outcome should be. This is not to say, of course, that physicians and healers of all types should not be using their intelligence; quite the contrary. The intellect is a powerful tool which should be developed as fully as possible and brought to bear whenever needed. The trick, however, is to learn to put it in the service of an open and loving heart. The more we can align the strength of our intellect, the control of our life-force energy, and a heart in harmony with Supreme Will, then the greater power we have to bring ourselves and others into a greater wholeness; which is true healing.'

"Although an extraordinary healer herself, Andora showed as much interest and enthusiasm in Zarmano's discussion as if she were hearing it for the first time. When he finished she asked if I wished to tour *the estate*.

"*The estate* was quite large, and to the casual observer, an exquisite stretch of rolling land, verdant slopes, plants of all varieties, and pathways that followed winding streams, then crossed them with charming wooden bridges and delicately-carved handrails. Majestic shade trees gave an air of ancient nobility, and nurtured exotic birds whose delightful sounds entertained all around like court musicians at a dance. Beyond the reaches where the merry popping of bubbling streams could be heard stood marble fountains whose splashing water sounded percussion for the birds' melodies. Rare flowers permeated the air with intoxicating aromas and dazzled the eye with brilliant hues that radiated rainbow-like in response to the dance of the sun's rays. The pervading harmony fostered a tranquillity that allowed all in its embrace to open up to healing.

"The true magic of *the estate,* however, was not to be found in this visible and exalted display. Scattered throughout were areas of special repose that took their occupants on unique journeys. Guided to these areas by the layout of the estate, and embraced by the serenity it induced, visitors entered these theaters—as they amusingly came to be called—to view scenes they had always refused to see. Each film, therefore, was unique, and came directly from each person's own experiences. For example, in the driving desire to get ahead, how did a person's ambition affect what happened to others? Other scenes may show the effects of the viewer's lack of thought or consideration for someone else. It is quite common for people to be so self-centered that they just have no notion about the consequences of their actions. Or they may be totally unaware of the way their lack of an appropriate response may be hurtful to others.

"'Depending on the nature of their actions,' Andora now picked up the discussion where Zarmano had left off, 'viewers would see different things. In every case, however, they would come to realize that all our actions have real consequences, not only for ourselves, but for others as well. There was no limit to the scenes one could see. The only *requirement* was that viewers finally understood and became so truly moved by what they saw, that they began to lament their actions and wish they had done things differently. It was clear when this point was reached because they revealed a real shift in their energy. A space in their heart opened—often for the first time—and allowed them to be moved by a compassion they had never known.

"'Sometimes it seems certain people have led exemplary lives, have always been kind, considerate, and loving, then some tragic illness befalls them. It almost seems as though they are being punished for something not of their doing. This is always very difficult to say, however. One never knows how exemplary a person's life has really been, nor what karmic forces still affect outcomes. Nevertheless illness is never about punishment anyway. It is really about having the opportunity to step back from our daily routine, examine ourselves in greater depth and with a new perspective, see how our lives have affected others and in what ways, see how responsive we have been toward others, and finally, know what we need to change in order to grow into the greater wholeness of ourselves. Moreover we have an opportunity in our illnesses to be a teacher to others; to show them how we can handle such a condition with dignity and respect for the learning our illnesses can provide, and how we can be moved to open up into greater awareness, love, and compassion; in short move into our greater wholeness.

"'Whether our illnesses accompany our bodies out of existence or we're restored to better physical health is less important than the positive impact the illness has been able to have on both the ill and the well. If the illness is able to bring awareness to the ill that one or more aspects of their lives is either detrimental to their total well-being, or that they have the capacity to become even more than they were before the illness, yet they refuse the invitation and continue their lives just as before, then they have essentially wasted a great opportunity. This may be a strategy some may adopt as a stubborn way to demonstrate that nothing—including illness—is going to defeat or get the better of them; a way to prove their mettle. They might just as well have said that if they have to go to school they're going to refuse to learn. The fact is that illness can be a lesson in life's schoolroom. And even if people learn their lessons on their death beds, then they are just that much more ahead in their psychic bodies after death and in subsequent incarnations.

"'Even if people do not believe in any continuity of their existence it is still important to be open to the inherent teaching capacity of illness. For one thing, they never quite know the outcome. Many people demonstrate remarkable recoveries after their physicians' dire pronouncements. This often happens precisely because they open up to the lesson involved and allow it to move them into greater wholeness. This is healing at a deep level, restoring the body to a level of balance and harmony in which the physical symptoms no longer have a foothold, or a need to express themselves, thereby disappearing and resulting in cure. Even if this is not the eventual outcome, at what point in a person's life can anyone say that learning is no longer possible or desirable? If anything, just taking the approach that one is always open to learning and moving into greater wholeness can be an inspirational and important lesson for all those around the dying person.

"'Illness, then, is one of the great transformers of our existences. Everything that we do in life is an opportunity to respond to ourselves and to others. Every moment is an opportunity to stop the random firing of countless and generally meaningless thoughts and become aware of the Great Spirit manifesting Itself in our being. Every action can be accented in kindness and clothed in compassion. But ask yourselves how often you do this in the daily course of your lives. Not uncommonly in modern society people race around from one task to another, often performing multiple tasks simultaneously, and with a constant running of concerns in their heads. The idea of stopping all this and stepping back, even for brief moments, is absurd and unthinkable for most; even on vacation time! In fact even in times of illness some people will still resist the opportunity that's been given them to stop the merry-go-round and look into the stuff of their lives.

"'This is not to say that people should seek out illness as an opportunity to stop the treadmill. The reason that illness is such a great opportunity is because it is no picnic. It is an experience associated with deep pain, fear, insecurity, loneliness, financial hardship, worry, and uncertainty. In fact it is precisely because it can be so devastating that it has the power to move past and knock down the inner walls, blocks, and other obstacles people have built up over the course of their lives. It then forces us to ask: Is there another way? In other words, can people move into greater wholeness without getting some terrible illness? Of course it is possible, and many have done it and continue to engage in those practices that foster it. They are, as you know, Narada, from your talks with Carana, Ardana, and others, such things as meditation, conscious breathing, energy techniques, and mindfulness.'

"Throughout Andora's discussion we traversed *the estate,* and let the encompassing serenity serve as a canvas for the scenes of healing and illness she painted on it. After we had strolled for a time in silence she suggested I might like to enter one of the *theaters* and see which of my own scenes played back for me. I quickly tried to rummage through the contents of my life to anticipate what I might find, but I never expected to go back before that!

"I entered with some slight trepidation, but quickly relaxed into a cushioned seat that perfectly conformed itself to the contours of my body. Without having to touch, turn, or activate anything I immediately found myself encased in something perhaps best described as an energy tunnel. Everything around me faded into a blur as the surrounding energy rotated with accelerating speed, accompanied by a low whirring sound that increased in pitch. I have no idea how long this process lasted because it seemed as though the energy vortex created a vacuum that sucked my consciousness right out of my body.

"When I came back into body consciousness, I found myself lying propped up in a sick bed like an ill patient, in a room full of flowing fabric of intricate paisley prints. I was well attended and visitors kept coming to see me, all bearing gifts and a similar message.

"'Oh, Sri Sankara, my divine mother/father and keeper of my faith. Thank you for your continued blessings and prayers. Thank you for the compassion and kindness you impart even through your own suffering and pain. Thank you for your example, and may I be as strong should I so suffer illness.'

"It is I who offer thanks to you, my faithful. I live through your faith, and my joy in your belief overcomes any pain I might otherwise feel. Take my blessings, for they shall live on after I leave this body, and take into your heart the same joy that is also my medication. I shall never forget you, but be ever ready to respond to your suffering whenever I hear my name called. Go now, in peace of mind and body, knowing that you are my cure and comfort.

"After my attendant ushered this last visitor out of my room, she asked if I needed anything else then left me to rest and prepare for a sermon I was to give that evening. I leaned back against the bed and began to feel as though the whole room were spinning around me. I began to wonder if my *time* had come, when the process that brought me there reversed itself and I found myself back in *the estate theater.*

"It took me some moments to settle down and gather myself. Andora and Zarmano were both there waiting for me, amused by the look of uncertainly that played across my face. 'Are you suffering from jet lag, Narada? You certainly crossed a lot of time zones!' Zarmano's joke made them both laugh and made me feel more comfortable. I told them how the scene from my last life-time stirred up a lot of memories and brought home to me the power of what Andora had said about being a teacher and positive influence on others even in the midst of a serious illness. I was also very moved by the fact that I had played such a central role in the lives of so many and had been able to bring so much caring and comfort to them.

"'And this is *not* something,' Andora continued, 'that only an advanced and accomplished teacher and sage as yourself is capable of doing. Many people heal into such an expansive wholeness as a result of their illness that they inspire and invite others to expand into their own wholeness. Your own experience was particularly influential because of so many people's lives you touched; people who looked up to you and regularly sought your guidance and wisdom.'

"We left that spot where we had just spent some time and continued to stroll through the estate. No one said anything which was perfect for me as my mind remained engaged with thoughts and memories of my life as Sankara. So many people had I met in my current lifetime who seemed so familiar to me; people who I felt I knew upon meeting for the first time; people with whom I connected instantly in a deep and intimate way, emotionally and spiritually—is it possible that we had been together at that ashram in India 200 years ago? Or perhaps during some lifetime even long before that? It was certainly true that at an earlier time I had been with Andora, Zarmano, Carana, Ardana, and the others; in fact, as they pointed out, numerous times before. Then it certainly made sense that the reason these others with whom I connected so easily and naturally is because we, too, had previously been associated in some capacity and probably many times before. As my internal musings continued my outer sight did not register anything. My reverie was eventually broken, however, when Zarmano spoke again.

"'Narada, I don't want you to miss this particular area.'

"I shifted my focus and realized we had come to a place unlike anything I had yet seen on *the estate*. It was a circular area, perhaps twenty-five feet in diameter, lined with tall trees that formed a natural canopy over the interior. I asked my guides if this was some sort of meeting place, and they suggested we enter. Inside, another circle was formed by a ring of chairs, which were unlike any I had ever seen. Each one seemed to grow right out of the ground like a bush, yet the surface had the texture of velvet. Moreover, each chair perfectly supported the body and conformed to every shift it made. Inside this circle was a fountain, although not the typical male fountain in which water shoots out of the ground. This was a female fountain, in which water entered from the sides, swirled around, and poured down a hole in the middle. We sat down, not next to each other, but across from each other, so that our placement formed a triangle.

"It was extremely pleasant and relaxing being there. The trees provided a sense of protection and created a very intimate and safe space. The sound of the water blocked out all other sounds and drew our focus toward the hole in the center. The effect was mesmerizing. As I continued to stare at it I felt my consciousness leaving my body and merging with the swirling water. I also felt the presence of Andora and Zarmano moving with me. Together we swirled into the hole and descended into a deep and dark tunnel. Down, down, down we dropped, a liquid energy of consciousness.

"Finally we drained out into a pool that lay inside a domed building, built entirely of crystal. Like a laser beam of light, the sun came through the dome, and when it passed prism-like through a particular part of the crystal, a rainbow of colors struck the water. As the sunlight continued to move over the crystal the

that person. Similarly the degree to which we can have a relationship with an object depends on our ability to connect with it. Some of the things you have seen us do, which others would see as extraordinary feats, are possible because of the intimate identification and connection we have, not only with the atomic structure of nature, but, even more importantly, with their more fundamental and underlying force fields. We are no longer bound by the same confines of time and matter that limit most people. Nevertheless the so-called amazing things we do have been accomplished by others for thousands of years. Even today increasing numbers of people are realizing more and more of their innate potential. As practices such as meditation increase, and people go further inside to the source of their being, they often startle themselves with the discovery of new powers and insights.

"'In order for us to have come back here we had to connect our minds and bodies. That allowed us the capability to dissolve the barriers locking consciousness into body, mind, matter, and time. Narada, you had an experience many years ago that approached this. Do you remember?'

"I searched my memory files under 'unusual,' 'unsolved,' even 'bizarre,' but couldn't seem to locate it. It occurred—Andora had to remind me—while I was living in another country; which is where I must have filed it. I was walking through a chaotic section of the city when all of a sudden I shifted into an altered state of consciousness. When people started walking right up to me, then through me, I realized I had become invisible. I moved effortlessly through the crowd, not having to dodge anybody. I was aware at the time, and for some time afterwards, that something extraordinary had happened. Yet after a while, with nothing seemingly to 'hang it on,' I decided I must have had some type of dream hallucination and just stopped thinking about the event. Now, after all these years, it came alive for me in a new way.

"Andora started to comment on it when Arzano and Manora arrived. They motioned for us to go on, but Andora and I communicated in a look that we would take up the discussion another time. Now, we all just agreed to break for the day. The others arrived shortly thereafter, and we began another evening of food, fun, and entertainment.

Chapter Nine

A Precious Gift

"The following morning I went to the temple as usual wondering who might be there to greet and instruct me. I was somewhat surprised, therefore, to find the place empty. I had by now learned they have jobs all over the world and often deal with people in all kinds of crises. For this reason I wasn't particularly concerned. It was actually kind of nice to be alone for a while. Food was on the table waiting for me, so I ate leisurely, letting my mind wander before deciding what I might do next. As I was finishing my meal my eyes strayed over to the meditation area where I had been only that one time with Balcano. I decided this would be a great place to do my morning meditation.

"For some strange reason I approached it slowly and with a mindful excitement. The place had held an inchoate, yet ancient fascination for me from the moment I arrived; although no opportunity had ever prevailed to bring me there alone till now. Like metal entering a magnet's field of attraction, I was pulled to the meditation area by some unknown force. As I entered I experienced a tingling sensation pulsing through my body that felt like tiny currents of electricity. I had already entered an altered state of consciousness by the time I began the meditation.

"As soon as I sat down and closed my eyes a powerful bolt of energy shot up from the earth, into my root chakra, up my spine, and out the top of my head. Then, as if floodgates had been opened up, the energy maintained its flow in this same manner with a steady force. Like a neon tube that begins to glow as it's charged with electricity, I began to feel myself glowing, radiating a transparent and scintillating light. I felt an overwhelming sense of deep and compassionate love and joy that moved me both to tears and laughter. At a certain point I opened my eyes, almost as if expecting my light to be real and illuminating the walls. What I saw instead, however, amazed me beyond comprehension.

"While I noticed the walls had indeed become illuminated, it appeared to be coming from another source. There, on the wall, completely covering the whole curved section, were large radiant symbols that seemed to be grouped into words, lines, and stanzas. It seemed to be a poem written in some language I didn't know, yet as I continued to stare, I began to recognize it, and the message formed clearly in my mind.

I Am the breeze that blows through the memories of
     your lives;
the light bursting from your core.
The stars whose twinkle reflects your delight,
I Am all these, yet so much more.

I Am the moon that remembers your mood;
the one, Yes! it's you I adore.
And the dread that yearns for expression in you,
I Am these too, yet so much more.

I Am the air whose breath gives you life;
the soul that cries out to soar.
The timid, the bold, without end can be told,
I Am all these, yet so much more.

I Am the stream that collects all your lives;
the One also known as the Door,
Beyond which you'll find the goal of your search.
I Am this, yet so much more.

Beyond the clouds and outer galaxies,
in the infinite space between each atom,
I Am the same throughout the ages.
No amount, equals my sum.

I am the thread, life's web my fabric;
the needle guiding it through.
My patterns are infinite, my colors Divine.
I Am the One throughout your lives, the One you always
     knew.

As oft' times before, you'll know me again;
shadows disperse when you open your eyes.
I Am the One who'll be waiting for you
unlike before with no other disguise.

"I continued to stare at the poem, mentally articulating its meaning over and over in my head. All of a sudden my attention was drawn to the meditation circle. From each sitting area, save one, there appeared a strange configuration of energy waves, like you see emanating from the hot pavement of a road when viewed from the right angle. The waves grew stronger and more vibrant, slowly forming into the most gossamer and shimmering film of light. Before their human features even became apparent, I *saw* before me Carana, Ardana, Jandara, Manora, Zarmano, Balcano, Belanin, Andora, Rolana, and Arzano.

"Each appeared around the meditation circle fully illuminating the whole temple with the radiant light beaming around their bodies. Carana then addressed me. 'You know, I'm sure, where that poem comes from?'

"'Well, I believe I wrote it, but how did it get on the wall? Also, why did you all appear just now?'

Carana continued to respond to my questions. "'Narada, you wrote this poem on this very spot where we now sit. In fact this area became your favorite place for sitting in meditation. You discovered—although I don't think you ever realized it—one of the earth's power points; part of its subtle *anatomical* structure, if you will, of acupressure lines and points. We, ourselves, didn't realize the significance of this spot until after you left us. When we did, we decided to build our temple right here with this meditation area centered directly over this point. In honor to your memory we inscribed your poem into the wall.'

"'Why, then,' I asked, 'did I not see it until now?'

"'Nor any of us. We didn't inscribe it by chiseling it into the wall. Instead we figured out a unique way of putting it there in which it would only come to life—that is become visible—as a result of being sufficiently charged up with your energy. We knew that whenever that moment came it would be significant, because it would signify your having attained a particular level of conscious awareness. We have waited a long time for this. We decided that we would all re-assemble for the occasion, regardless of where we might be at the time, although we knew this week the moment was imminent.'

"'What is this language the poem is written in?' I asked Carana.

"'This is Sanskrit. We all knew the language having been students of the ancient Hindu texts. It is not surprising, therefore, that you became Sankara in your subsequent life and continued your teachings in that area.'

"Carana stopped speaking, and for a while an intense stillness wrapped its protective embrace around us. It was a brief moment of infinite time, in which the bonds of intimacy created over thousands of years and innumerable lifetimes condensed into a tiny particle of explosive potential. The space then deferentially yielded its silent authority to Ardana, whose sweetness and tenderness always and unexpectedly expressed the power and command of a sovereign. I felt a foreboding tug on my emotional heartstrings before she even began to speak.

"'Narada, this event is significant in another way as well. By now you have been with and received special instruction from everyone of us.'

"I immediately but respectfully interrupted her, perhaps out of apprehension of what she was going to say, and also in an effort to prolong my interactions with them. 'Ardana,' I said, 'I still haven't been with Belanin.' I was not inclined to be amusing at that point, but they all laughed. Then Belanin, himself, addressed me in a tone of sweet jesting.

"'Narada, don't you remember when I was with you?'

"They all looked at me with expectant gazes that expressed both their surprise as well as delight. Belanin continued.

"'Just after you arrived, Narada, you had a dream in which you were on a long journey, on the train. You were staring out the window when a stranger appeared across from you. It was a stranger to you in more ways than one—not quite human, but with a transparent surface from which pulsating beams of light emanated. Do you remember? That was I. I then guided you through the rest of your dream, in which you came across your beloved Adonara. Then do you remember when you took that trip with Manora and Arzano down into town? After you were all seated in the central square for a while they left you to go meet a friend. Right after that, some foul-smelling miscreant—which is how you thought of him—came up and sat down next to you. His annoying behavior soon turned threatening and had you running through the town and the fields.'

"'Don't tell me that was also you!' I exclaimed. I dove into a pensiveness that tried to capture those moments and re-assess them with my new knowledge. I didn't get very far when Ardana pulled me out of it.

"'So, as I said, Narada, you have now spent some very special and individual time with all of us. Now you must return to your home. It is our greatest wish that you will seek out Adonara and bring her back here with you. That will also help fulfill our ultimate destiny. However this is something you must pursue with a free will and determination. We will always be with you, just as we have always been with you. You also know you can contact, as well as visit us, whenever you need or want to.'

"I remained motionless with a mixture of sadness and excitement. While I didn't want to leave, I really desired to find Adonara and help bring our whole family back together again. Then Carana spoke again.

"'Before you return, Narada, we have something very special to give you.'

"As he spoke these words I became aware of something materializing on my lap. Eleven sets of eyes fixated on one spot. The object materialized slowly, as though to increase the drama and suspense of the occasion. Finally I held in my hands the most exquisite golden flute I had ever seen. I trembled, as it shook me to the core of my being. Strange sensations flooded my body, and I was too overcome to speak.

"'Do you remember this flute?' Carana asked me. 'Adonara had it made for you by our finest goldsmith. Then for twenty-four days she infused it with energy and blessings. She conducted special rituals over it and had it blessed by the Earth Goddess and the Sun Goddess. This is, in fact, the instrument you were playing that summoned our Supreme Goddess, just before you and Adonara plummeted to your deaths.'

"'How, then, did you get the flute after that?' I asked him.

"'Well, we were all so shaken up and traumatized by the blast that at first we didn't even think of the flute. When we were able to collect our thoughts somewhat, we just assumed it remained buried with you at the bottom of the mountain. At some later time we went back to that area to inspect the damage. A bright gleaming caught our eyes, and at first we thought that the blast had opened up a vein of gold. It turned out to be your flute. Apparently it must have flown out of your hands at the impact of the explosion. We have been looking forward a long time to give it back to you. It is still infused with the magic and blessings of its creators; apparently much stronger than even that great explosion that sent you on your way.'

"'What exactly is its power?' I asked.

"'That is something you must discover for yourself, because it is only how you use and interact with it that its power will be revealed.'

"We ended that day with a special celebration, and the next day they helped me plan my departure."

Epilogue

All of a sudden I was startled to hear the conductor call out over the speaker system the last stop. I opened my eyes, looked up, and in the absence of anybody else in my compartment, I realized I was, and had been throughout the whole trip, alone! My confusion was quickly diverted, however, by something I felt lying across my lap that hadn't been there earlier. I looked down and saw the golden flute that had been given to Narada.

I ended my journey only to realize I had actually arrived at the beginning.